MINT TEA AND A MIDSUMMER MURDER

A WATERWHEEL CAFE MYSTERY

VICTORIA TAIT

KANGA PRESS

Cover Design by Daniela Colleo of StunningBookCovers.com
Editing Allie Douglas

For more information visit VictoriaTait.com

CHAPTER ONE

Thirty-four-year-old Sergeant Keya Varma turned up the volume of her car radio and enthusiastically sang along to Katrina and the Waves' *Walking on Sunshine,* playing on the local Corinium Radio station.

Sunlight filtered through the leaves of an avenue of tall, green-leafed beech trees, creating pools of light on the tarmac road.

It was mid-June, but summer had come slowly to the Cotswolds this year. After some fine weather in April, May had been a disappointing washout, and even the beginning of June had been damp and grey. But now, as the summer solstice and Midsummer's Day approached, the sun was shining, and the temperature was finally rising.

Keya sped along in her police Ford Focus, with its distinctive blue and yellow markings, to the wonderfully named villages of Lower, Little and Great Rollright on the northerly edge of the Cotswolds, to meet members of the Rollright Trust.

Spotting a car pulling out of a lay-by up ahead, she slowed down and parked beside the busy country road, which was a cut through between the A436 and A3400.

Using the rearview mirror, she adjusted her flat black hat with its black and white chequerboard band, before picking up her pen and notebook. She checked her phone, but there was no signal at this high point of the Cotswolds.

She had arrived at The Rollright Stones, an ancient monument dating back thousands of years.

When she'd first been contacted to provide advice in her role as the Cotswolds' Rural Engagement Officer, she'd been surprised to learn of a stone circle in the same vein as Stonehenge in her area. But as she emerged from a small coppice beside a field of green stalked wheat, she gazed disappointedly at a ring of irregular shaped stones, none of which was more than a metre tall.

It was a far cry from the one time she'd visited Stonehenge. Its huge rectangular rocks, some of which balanced on top of others, left visitors marvelling and wondering how the ancient druids had created the sacred monument without modern-day cranes and lifting equipment.

"Sergeant Varma?" called an authoritative male voice.

She turned and watched as a man and a woman approached along the track beside the wheat field. Both were of retirement age, but they made an odd couple.

In spite of the balmy weather, the man was wearing a tweed suit and a brown trilby hat, and he marched along despite his slight stoop. The curly, grey-haired woman, who scuttled to keep up with him, was painfully thin. She was wearing a plum-coloured skirt, which reached to her calves, and a pair of solid walking boots, with thick red socks poking out of the tops of them. She was carrying a wicker basket.

"I'm Dr Reid," the man announced as he reached Keya and held out his hand.

Keya shook it and found the doctor's grip firm but the gesture fleeting.

"Chairman of the Standing Stones Heritage Committee, and this is our secretary, Dora Potts."

"Hello," Dora replied, smiling at Keya. "It's awfully kind of you to meet us like this."

"It's what she's paid to do," snapped the doctor.

"Yes, of course, Silas," Dora muttered, glancing apologetically at her companion.

"Right. Summer Solstice. The bane of our committee's existence," began Dr Reid.

"Shouldn't we wait for Aurora?" Dora suggested hesitantly.

"If she can't be here on time, she can't expect to have a view," declared Dr Reid as he removed his hat and fanned his reddening face.

"Cooee. I'm not late, am I?" a voice called, and Keya turned towards the edge of the wheat field and watched a brightly clad woman emerge through a metal kissing gate.

"No, Aurora, we haven't started yet," Dora called back.

The round, red-faced woman stopped and placed her hands on her ample hips and breathed in deeply. At least she was dressed for the weather, if not for walking, with a flowing gypsy-style skirt of blues and purples and a tasselled loose pink top.

As she walked slowly towards them, she grumbled, "It always takes me longer to walk up the hill from the village than I think. And I've been busy serving customers this morning."

Dora turned to Keya and explained, "Aurora runs the popular Standing Stones shop in the village."

"And I also give tarot card readings, should you like one, Officer," Aurora added.

"Can we get down to business?" Dr Reid cut in.

"Yes, of course," Dora apologised, drawing her lips together and bowing her head.

Aurora proclaimed, "I believe this year's solstice should be all about balance, and nature, and finding joy and happiness in the world around us."

"Oh, yes," Dora agreed, looking up.

A figure of a young woman floated out of the coppice of trees. Keya blinked and refocused, wondering if the spirituality of her surroundings was playing tricks on her.

"What's she doing here?" hissed Aurora.

"Ah, Daisy. You're just in time," called Dr Reid.

"Silas thought we ought to involve the mill. Sir Anthony wasn't interested, and Theo was busy, so he suggested Daisy join us. Like you, she's also into nature and paganism."

Aurora's nostrils flared and her eyes flashed, but by the time the younger, thinner, and prettier Daisy joined them, Aurora had composed herself.

"If I'd known you were coming, Daisy, we could have walked here together," Aurora said with false sincerity.

Daisy smiled and replied, "Actually, I had a delivery for the Knights Farm Shop, which is why I'm late. But I did speak to Mr Graham, and he's agreed that visitors to the summer solstice can park at the farm shop. In fact, he's rather enthusiastic about the event and started talking about providing picnics, and a special midsummer breakfast. And we can use his facilities. There's even a shower if people don't mind paying a couple of pounds to use it."

"Well done, my dear." Dr Reid placed a hand on the top of her arm.

Daisy tensed and stepped towards the circle of stones.

"Shall we have the skull in the centre, like last year?" she asked with her back to the group. Her fair hair was long, reaching nearly to her narrow waist, and it was streaked with blonde. She was wearing a simple summer dress with capped sleeves.

"I thought we should revert to tradition and have a bonfire," Aurora replied.

Dr Reid looked stricken. "A bonfire. In the middle of the standing stones?"

"Not a huge one, but the ancients believed that the heat of the fire boosted the strength of the sun for the remainder of the growing season and ensured a healthy harvest. And after all the rain last month, the crops need some encouragement."

"That's what Theo said. I know he's worried about low yields this year," Daisy said, turning to face them.

"There are plenty of fallen branches after that storm last month," Dora agreed. "I've been meaning to come and clear them up."

In the gap in the conversation, Keya asked, "And what assistance do you want from the police?"

"I'm not sure we do now," Dr Reid replied. "I was concerned about parking and potential accidents as people loitered on the road, but Daisy has solved that problem for us."

Daisy inclined her head.

"Talk me through how it works," said Keya.

"It's such a spiritual event. You should join us," enthused Aurora.

"Thanks, but I already have tickets to watch *A Midsummer Night's Dream* at the Rococo Gardens, in Painswick," Keya replied.

Her friend, Dotty, had suggested the outdoor theatre event. Constable Ryan Jenkins, her younger colleague at Cirencester Police Station, had enthusiastically agreed that he and his now confirmed girlfriend, Millie, who worked in Keya's cafe, would love to go. And they'd persuaded Keya to join them.

It wasn't that Keya didn't like plays. She just didn't have time to find out what was on and organise going to see anything. But now Dotty was living back in the area, they'd probably attend more local events.

"Theo's taking me there on Saturday. It's supposed to be very good," Daisy said.

Dr Reid cleared his throat. "People start arriving in the early evening, to see the standing stones and to visit the Whispering Knights tomb on the far side of the field," he said, bringing the subject back to the summer solstice event.

"And they have picnics, and play music, and create flower wreaths," added Aurora.

"Any drugs?" Keya asked.

"There is drinking," Dora replied. "I have to tidy up the bottles and other rubbish after they leave."

Dr Reid coughed. "The sun is due to set at ten to ten and rise again on the longest day, the 21st June, at ten to five. There are those who spend all night at the stones, and others who turn up just for the sunrise. We get rid of most of them by seven."

"Don't be so fractious, Silas," Aurora remonstrated. "It's a joyful event steeped in folklore and mythology which spans back centuries. We should be grateful to the people who chose to build the stone circle here."

"Because it provides you with a healthy income," retorted the doctor.

"And I'm not the only one. Your wife's shop doesn't do too badly from the tourists, even if Daisy's bakery has drawn away many of the lunchtime passers-by."

Keya, whose mind had been drifting off to images of scantily clad people dancing around a fire wearing floral garlands, started. "You make bread?" she asked Daisy.

Daisy nodded. "It was Theo's idea to showcase the heritage grains he uses at the mill. But as well as the bread, we've found sandwiches are very popular, particularly in the summer, and we also bake cakes and scones."

"And you deliver?"

"We've just started supplying local pubs and restaurants, who prefer to outsource to us rather than making their own bread."

"I run a cafe, at Coln Akeman. I'd love to see what you do."

Daisy smiled invitingly. "Why not follow me back to the village, and I'll make you a sandwich for your lunch?"

CHAPTER TWO

"Could I trouble you for a lift, Officer?" Aurora asked. "I really should get back to the shop. I've left my friend, Viv, in charge. She's a palm reader, you know. Descended from true Romany gypsies."

Keya had said goodbye to Dr Reid and Dora, and she was following Daisy back to the road through the coppice of trees as Aurora babbled on beside her.

She wasn't really supposed to give people lifts in her police vehicle, but she supposed it would be OK to run Aurora down to Lower Rollright. She was going that way to visit Daisy's bakery, and as Aurora gripped the handle of the passenger door, she didn't think she'd be able to refuse.

Keya watched Daisy approach a small cream van parked in what she presumed was a second lay-by.

"You'll need to turn round," Aurora said, as they both climbed into the police car and Keya turned on the engine.

A few minutes later, Keya was following Daisy's van downhill and as they entered the village of Lower Rollright, a low stone wall appeared on their right.

"That's where Sir Anthony lives," Aurora explained. "He owns the mill, and he ran it with his brother until a few years ago when his nephew, Theo, short for Theodore, arrived and shook things up."

Keya wondered how he had shaken things up, but she didn't get a chance to ask.

"And that is Debbie Reid's Village Stores."

After several smart properties, partially hidden by high hedges, they passed a row of terraced houses and, occupying two of them, was the Rollright Village Store. Its green canopy shaded two pairs of green chairs, placed either side of small square tables.

Lower Rollright was a typical Cotswold village. The buildings were constructed from distinctive honey-coloured stone and between them were neat gardens, healthy green hedges and mature trees. Several houses were decorated with hanging baskets or window box displays of bright, fresh flowers.

As they approached a stone bridge, beneath which Keya presumed there was a stream or small river, Daisy's cream van indicated left, and Keya followed it into a street running parallel with the watercourse. The first building on the right was the aptly named Malt Shovel pub.

"Here we are," Aurora announced.

Keya hesitated as the van continued straight along the narrow street.

"You can drop me here," Aurora insisted in a louder voice. "Daisy's bakery is only a few buildings further on." As Aurora said this, Keya saw the van indicate right and turn off the road.

Keya pulled to the side of the road, just beyond a purple-framed shop front.

"Do pop in after you've visited the bakery," Aurora said as she climbed out of the police car and slammed the door shut.

Charming, thought Keya. Not even a thanks for the lift.

Keya drove slowly forward and parked outside the cream-framed shopfront of the Stone Circle Bakery. The image sprayed on the shop window was a circle with three ears of wheat inside it.

A small bell tinkled as Keya entered the bakery and she heard Daisy call, "I'll be with you in a minute."

Keya breathed in the wonderful aroma of freshly baked bread. In front of her there was a glass counter with a display of sandwich fillings on one side and sweet treats on the other, including pieces of delicious-looking chocolate brownie, perfectly round fruit scones, and slices of a rich, dark cake topped with a fluffy sand-coloured icing.

To her left, there was a display of bread loaves of all different shapes and sizes arranged on sloping wooden shelves. And below them, several long white bread batons protruded from a wooden bucket.

"Welcome to our bakery," Daisy said as she tied the cord of a cream-coloured apron with Stone Circle Flour printed on it around her waist.

"All our bread is made from heritage grains," Daisy continued. "The mill has specialised in them ever since Theo took it over from his uncles. And he was right to do so, as they're now all the rage. We supply local restaurants, celebrity chefs, and artisan bakers all over the country."

As Daisy slipped on a pair of transparent gloves she said, "You really should try one of our trademark malthouse bread buns." She turned to the shelf behind her where baskets of bread buns were displayed. Some were plain on top, while others were decorated with different seeds.

"Do you like pumpkin seeds?" Daisy asked, her back to Keya as she reached into a basket.

"Yes," Keya replied, intrigued.

Daisy removed a bread bun with large oval seeds baked into the top of it. She turned round and placed it on a wooden bread board as she asked, "Which filling? The asparagus is fresh and grown locally, and it'll be your last chance to taste it as the season finishes at the summer solstice. It goes well with chicken or bacon."

"I'm a vegetarian," Keya replied.

"Then how about asparagus with a thin layer of cream cheese, a handful of fresh salad leaves, and a dollop of lemon mayonnaise?" Daisy smiled at Keya.

"That sounds wonderful."

As Daisy prepared the sandwich, Keya asked, "How long have you had the bakery?"

"Less than a year. It was Theo's idea to renovate the old blacksmith's shop and use the bakery to showcase Stone Circle Flour. But we didn't expect it to be so popular."

"Theo is Sir Anthony's nephew?" Keya clarified.

"Yes. His full name is Theodore Watson, and his mum is Sir Anthony's sister. He knew absolutely nothing about milling when he arrived, but he'd been involved with several successful start-up businesses. One of them uses the waste bits of potatoes to make fibres. It's what all the company's T-shirts and aprons are made from. We sell them here, too."

Daisy glanced over Keya's shoulder and Keya turned round to view a display of Stone Circle merchandise occupying the space on the opposite side of the shop. More wooden shelves were attached to the front wall, holding packets of flour, and there were large flour sacks resting on the floor beneath them.

Keya turned back to the counter and said, "So you and Theo are business partners?"

"Oh, no. The mill pays me to run the bakery, but it's fun. And I like working with Theo."

Keya hesitated. Daisy seemed open and honest, but Keya thought it intrusive to ask if there was more to her relationship with Theo. Instead, she enquired, "Do you live in the village?"

"Yes, Theo and I have a house just past the mill. It's always been the manager's house, and Theo likes to be close to his work."

"So you live together?" Keya was still intrigued by the couple's relationship.

"Yes, ever since my dad kicked me out. He doesn't approve of Theo."

"Really?" Surely Daisy's father would be delighted that she was with the manager of a successful local business.

"Yes, because Theo's thirty-six and I'm twenty-four. My dad thought I should stick to boys my own age." Daisy sighed as she added mixed lettuce leaves to the sandwich.

Behind her, Keya heard the shop bell tinkle.

"You're not in any trouble, are you, Daisy?" asked a concerned young male voice.

"Don't be daft, Ash. This is … oh, I don't know your name," Daisy looked apologetically at Keya.

Keya stepped to one side so she could address both Daisy and the new arrival, who was a skinny, shaven-headed young man dressed all in black apart from a grey Stone Circle T-shirt. "Sergeant Keya Varma, Rural Engagement Officer for the Cotswolds."

Daisy explained to Ash, "Dr Reid's worried about the summer solstice, so he'd arranged a meeting for us all, but I think we sorted everything out. Knights Farm Shop is going to let people park there, which should stop them from parking on the road."

"I don't know what all the fuss is about," Ash muttered.

"But you always go. And it's such a wonderful, spiritual event. Watching the sunrise over the Cotswolds."

"Do you have that delivery for The King's Head?" asked Ash.

"Just give me a minute." Daisy placed a brown paper bag on the counter which contained Keya's sandwich.

As Keya reached for it, Daisy gave her a larger bag and said, "Pick a loaf to take back and try too."

"Are you sure?"

"Of course. And we'd love to talk to you about supplying your cafe."

As Keya considered the bread loaves, Ash said, "And your mother asked me to pick her up a sandwich and a loaf of bread."

"I don't suppose she gave you any money to pay for them," Daisy responded. Her voice had an uncharacteristic edge of irritation to it.

"What do you think? But she did give me this bottle of her special hot sauce for you."

Daisy's voice softened. "That was thoughtful of her."

Having chosen and bagged her loaf, Keya turned and smiled at Daisy as she picked up the bag containing her sandwich. "Thanks for these."

"You're welcome. And if you do change your mind about the summer solstice, you can join Theo and me at the standing stones."

As she left the shop to the tinkling of the bell, Keya thought she heard Ash say, "I suppose I'll come too."

CHAPTER THREE

Keya left Lower Rollright and drove through the town of Chipping Norton before turning south and heading towards Coln Akeman.

Forty-five minutes later, she parked in a gravel area at the side of another flour mill. This was a disused one which had been converted into Akemans Antique Centre and at the rear, beside the mill's renovated waterwheel, was Keya's Waterwheel Cafe.

It was nearly a year since she'd opened it with the help of the manager of the antique centre, Gilly Wimsey.

Gilly was a motherly type with a ready smile who always had a kind or encouraging word. But as Keya collected her bag, sandwich, and the loaf of bread from her car, she wondered what her orange-haired friend was doing walking about barefoot on the grass above the bank which sloped down to the River Coln.

Keya walked down the flagstone path which had recently been laid to link the newly created gravel parking area with her delicatessen. Opened after the cafe, the small deli was located in a single-storey building adjacent to the cafe's external seating area. Beyond it was the three-storey mill building and the patio doors leading into the cafe.

As she walked, Keya kept glancing at Gilly, who was standing on one leg in a wobbly yoga pose, until she toppled over and planted both feet firmly on the ground.

"I'll have to have some of this asparagus," said a brightly clad figure, leaning over the rack of vegetables in a shaded section outside the deli. Keya knew from the voice and the bright yellow tunic top with purple flowers that the figure was Gilly's aunt, who everyone affectionally called Aunt Beanie.

Keya's youngest sister by fifteen years, Maitri, who ran the deli, said, "It's high quality even though it has to be sold as wonky. Apparently, the packing machine rejects anything that isn't a uniform size or shape, because the supermarkets won't accept it."

"Nature doesn't make things in uniform shapes and sizes," protested Aunt Beanie, "Even though you and your sisters would qualify as you're all thin and attractive."

"Thank you," responded Keya as she joined them.

Aunt Beanie looked up. She was wearing her trademark headscarf, which was purple today and tied with a huge bow at a jaunty angle on top of her head, holding back her long, grey hair. She was a tall, willowy figure with a forthright manner.

"What's Gilly doing?" asked Keya in a concerned voice.

"Grounding herself, literally," Aunt Beanie replied as Gilly toppled over from yet another attempt at a one-legged pose. "She's worried about turning fifty at the end of the month and is having an existential midlife crisis. I suggested that as summer has finally arrived, she should embrace nature, but I'm a little concerned about where that will lead." She tilted her head as she watched her niece.

Gilly was not one of nature's uniform figures. Not only did she have ringlets of bright orange hair, which clashed with her orange-framed glasses, she was definitely erring on the overweight side. But, Keya considered, when did Gilly have time to look after herself?

She was always busy sorting out some problem or welcoming a new trader to the antique centre. And she had two teenage children, Thomas and Olivia, and her husband, Peter, often worked antisocial hours as the area's local doctor.

Gilly saw them all staring at her and her face coloured, clashing with her hair. She called over, "I have to start somewhere!"

"How about with a cup of tea?" Keya called back. "We really need to discuss summer opening times and any special events for the cafe or antique centre."

"Oh, good idea." Gilly stepped into her shoes and walked across the grass to join them.

Keya removed the loaf of bread from its brown paper bag and said, "And we should try this. There's a new bakery in Lower Rollright, associated with the Stone Circle flour mill."

Maitri squeezed the loaf. "Firm, but not too much. Would they deliver? Lower Rollright is too far to go for bread."

"I think so, but probably not every day," Keya considered. "I'll cut you a slice and you can try it, but now I need to sit down with Gilly. Is there anything you want to raise with respect to the deli?"

Maitri looked towards Keya's police car and said, "The designated parking is already having a positive impact. When will the new signs arrive?"

"Next week," Gilly confirmed.

"How's the coffee machine?" asked Keya.

"It's great. And as we offer a discount if people use reusable cups rather than takeaway ones, we've sold quite a few waterwheel-branded thermal cups," Maitri replied. "And I chased up The Smiling Cow. They're a bit behind, but we should have our ice cream display and their stock by next week."

"That's good news," Keya replied.

"The whole enterprise is very innovative," declared Aunt Beanie. "And I love your new vegetable rack and the pre-packed local meats. It means I can pop in and buy everything I need for a meal. It's not just the luxury items anymore."

Maitri beamed. "That's what I'm hoping to do. Create a shop which is useful and convenient, as well as supplying tasty, quality, local items which aren't readily available in supermarkets."

Gilly and Keya left Aunt Beanie to choose her asparagus with Maitri. As they approached the cafe's patio doors, Keya's middle sister, Zivah, emerged pushing a compact black baby buggy.

"Sis," cried Keya. "I wasn't expecting you today."

"I needed to get out of the house, and the only time Kaami seems to sleep is in the car."

"May I?" asked Gilly, stepping forward and peering into the buggy.

"Oh, he's so cute," she marvelled. "I don't think Thomas was ever that tiny."

"And he's five weeks old now," Zivah said. "But it's hard for him to grow when he's constantly throwing up his milk."

"Colic," said Gilly.

"My doctor says not. I massage his tummy regularly, and Mum's tried a traditional Indian remedy of boiling up asafoetida and applying it to his belly button when it's cool, but he still cries for hours at night. And I don't know what I can do to help him."

Zivah looked exhausted and close to tears.

Gilly moved away from the pram and wrapped her arms around Zivah's thin frame.

Keya heard Zivah's sobs. But what could she do to help her sister?

CHAPTER FOUR

Keya left the cafe after helping with the lunchtime customers and arrived at Cirencester Police Station at three o'clock.

She walked into the team room to find her colleague, Ryan, Constable Jenkins, sitting at his desk talking to retired police sergeant, Stan Rowbottom.

"Your mum gave me this for you," Keya said as she placed a brown paper bag on Ryan's desk.

Ryan's mum, Monica, had taken over running the kitchen at the Waterwheel Cafe after Keya's mother had left to help Zivah with baby Kaami. Ryan's girlfriend, Millie, also worked at the cafe, and ran the front of house.

Ryan opened the top of the bag and peered in. Then he placed his hand inside, removed a round golden biscuit, and bit into it.

"Nice. Lemon curd flavour, I think. Very fresh."

Stan tasted a biscuit and nodded his head. "Moreish."

Ryan held the packet up to Keya.

"No, thanks. I ate a late lunch."

Keya's meeting with Gilly had been cut short by a coach load of tourists arriving to visit the antique centre, but they actually made a beeline for the cafe. Only after they, and the cafe's usual customers, had finished lunch did Keya try her sandwich. And it had been wonderfully fresh and tasty.

Everyone had been impressed by Daisy's bread. Monica and Millie thought Keya should consider it for the cafe sandwiches, and Maitri said she'd definitely be interested in stocking some in the deli.

"How was your meeting?" Ryan asked.

"Lots of hooded figures performing pagan rituals?" Stan enquired.

"It's nothing like that. And to be honest, I had the impression that some members of the committee which looks after the standing stones would rather the summer solstice event didn't happen at all."

"I don't blame them, but the stones are good business for such a rural area. Besides the Stone Circle Flour mill, there aren't many employment opportunities locally," Stan remarked with unusual seriousness.

The burly, brown-suited figure of Inspector Dai Evans entered the room. His round face was red-cheeked and stippled with broken veins, and his head was bald on top with short grey hair at the back and sides.

Tending towards sarcasm and crankiness, the recent loss of his mother had mellowed the inspector, and Keya often found him staring absently into space. She hated to wish for it, but he needed a major case to sink his teeth into.

"Afternoon, Sergeant. How were the Rollright loonies?"

"Sir! They're actually a very pleasant bunch, in the main. Somewhat eccentric, but that's not exactly unusual in the Cotswolds."

"Well it seems that the rise in temperature is getting to the residents. We have a road rage incident between a tractor and a Range Rover over in Guiting Power, and a shopkeeper has accused a tourist of shoplifting in Lower Slaughter and locked the offender in a toilet. I know we're short staffed, and you have plenty of work to do, Sergeant, but would you mind accompanying Constable Jenkins to check out these incidents? I don't think either of you should face the locals on your own when they're in this sort of mood."

Keya glanced across at the two empty desks in the team room. She and Ryan occupied desks facing each other, next to Inspector Evans' small office. Sujin, the station's crime scene technician, had insisted he didn't need a desk, as he spent all his time in his compact workroom next to the custody suite.

The other desk had been occupied by Inspector Sue, a family liaison officer, but she had retired and, although she now worked in a consultancy role, she had a desk elsewhere in the station.

"Chief Inspector Greg assures me he has applied to headquarters for at least one new member of our team. Hopefully, a constable who can take over from Constable Jenkins when he passes his sergeant's exams."

"No pressure there," muttered Stan, whose broom cupboard of an office was actually further along the corridor. He was in charge of files, but his extensive knowledge of people, places, and historic crimes was very useful to the team. As was his willingness to make hot drinks.

"Cuppa anyone?" asked Stan on cue.

CHAPTER FIVE

Keya and Ryan drove across the Cotswolds, chatting amicably and enjoying the views and the white, purple, and yellow wildflowers covering the verges. Ryan, who was driving, did complain though, "It's not easy to see traffic up ahead when the council leaves the verges untended."

"I suppose, like everything else, they don't have the money to spend on rural areas." Keya thought of her own position as the Cotswold's Rural Engagement Officer. It was technically a part-time role, yet she had over four hundred and fifty square miles of countryside to patrol and manage.

Thinking back to their discussion at the police station, Keya asked, "Are you worried about your sergeant's exams?"

"Yes. Everyone thinks I'll find them easy, but I won't. Computers, tech, and dismantling and rebuilding electrical items and the like, that I understand, but not exam papers. It was the same at school. English was my worst subject."

"Oh, you don't have to write long essays. It's all multiple-choice questions."

"Really? I didn't know that."

"Haven't you looked through your handbook?"

Ryan stared at the road in front of them. "No, I haven't got round to it," he said defensively.

Keya realised he really was worried about the autumn exam.

"I tell you what, why don't I sit down with you sometime and we can go through it? It's not nearly as scary as you think, and as your role is so wide, you'll instinctively know the answers to many of the questions. But you will need to read up on procedures and policies."

She decided to lighten the tone of the conversation, so she asked, "Have you and Millie recovered from last month's triathlon at the Cotswold Wildlife Park?"

"Oh yes. We were both fit, so we soon recovered."

"And do you have any more competitions lined up this month?"

"No. Our next one is in July in Cheltenham. So now the weather is better, we've decided to run the Cotswold Way."

"All of it?" Keya asked in surprise. She knew the trail consisted of over a hundred miles of tracks and footpaths following the edge of the Cotswold escarpment. It started in Bath, to the south, and finished in Chipping Campden, to the north. Even for Ryan and Millie, who were both extremely fit, it was a challenge.

"Not all at once," Ryan laughed. "Mum's going to drop us off in Bath on Sunday, before she goes to work at the cafe, and I'll leave my car in Wotton-under-Edge, so I can drive us home when we finish. That section is thirty-one miles. And we'll have all day so we can stop for breaks and even walk sections if we feel like it."

Even walk sections, thought Keya, shaking her head.

"Rather you than me. Dotty and I are going to Chipping Campden on Friday evening for their alternative Olympick Games. I thought you might be taking part in their running race?"

"I did think about it, but we decided to do the Cotswold Way instead. Are you or Dotty going to enter the shin-kicking?"

This version of sporting games dated back to the 1600s and some thought that William Shakespeare had once attended them when he'd been living not too far away in Stratford-upon-Avon. It involved an array of different competitions which anyone could enter.

Keya was disappointed when they reached the location of the reported road rage, as there were no vehicles in sight. They continued up the narrow, single-track road until they reached a farm. Spotting the farmer moving bales of hay with a forklift tractor from a trailer to a nearby barn, they decided to speak to him.

They drove into the farmyard, alongside a long single-storey stone building with a steep black slate roof and grey wooden support posts. There was an assortment of old garden furniture in the bays, along with rusting farm implements and stacks of colourful plastic animal feed bags.

"Aye, that was me," admitted the farmer when they questioned him about the reported incident. "The other bloke must have called you about it. He came tearing round a corner and nearly drove into me. Then he flashed his lights, expecting me to get out of his way. How could I? I was towing a trailer load of hay bales. So I just sat there and waited. He shouted some expletives at me, but nothing I haven't heard before."

The farmer removed his worn flat tweed cap and scratched his wispy brown hair. "Eventually he reversed back along the road, turned round in a field entrance and shot off back the way he'd come."

As they only had the farmer's account, and he seemed an honest type, they left him to finish unloading his hay bales and dismissed the incident.

Gilly Wimsey called as they were driving from Guiting Power to Lower Slaughter.

"I might lose you Gilly, as the phone signal is intermittent where we are," Keya told her friend and business colleague.

"I'll be quick. We didn't have a chance earlier to discuss the outdoor cinema event next month. The film company wants to know which film to allocate to us."

"What are the choices?" Keya asked.

Gilly and her family had attended a pop-up cinema screening the previous year, and Gilly had discovered that she could hire the company to provide a similar event at the cafe and antique centre.

They were going to hold it on the grassy area between the cafe's outside seating area and the deli, and the bank sloping down to the River Coln. Although the cafe would be open, they'd both agreed that visitors could bring their own picnics if they preferred, but alcoholic drinks had to be purchased from the cafe. Maitri also hoped to serve ice creams, as long as her display unit and stock had arrived in time.

Gilly said, "I've already rejected Pretty Woman, as I don't think its portrayal of women is appropriate, and I don't want Thomas getting ideas from Ferris Bueller's Day Off. I'm struggling to keep him at school as it is. But there is a sing-along version of *The Greatest Showman*. If we encourage people to dress up and ..." Gilly trailed off.

"That's a fabulous idea. I can't sing, but it'll still be fun. But aren't you concerned about circus costumes degrading women?"

"No, they're practical, and not everyone has to wear leotards and tights. I certainly won't!" Gilly said.

"Sing-along to *The Greatest Showman* it is then," Keya declared.

Her trip to Lower Slaughter with Ryan was just as unproductive as the one to Guiting Power. The shopkeeper was brusque and dismissed the shoplifting issue, saying that it had been resolved. She was extremely evasive when questioned about locking the suspect in a toilet. But as the suspect had left, with the rest of the tourists, there was nothing Keya or Ryan could do.

"Back to the station?" Ryan asked, sounding disappointed.

"I guess so," Keya replied.

But just as they were leaving Lower Slaughter, Keya's phone buzzed.

"Hiya, Stan," said Keya, answering the call.

"The inspector asked me to call you. There's been a report of a crop circle appearing near Cold Ashton, which is not too far from you, if you're still in Lower Slaughter."

"We've just left, but we can head over to Cold Ashton. What does the inspector want us to do?"

"Speak to the farmer whose field's been vandalised, create a report, and log it on the system. He's worried that now we have our first crop circle sighting, we'll have a spate of them turning up all over the area."

Keya finished the call and sighed. "Take the next right," she told Ryan. "We've been asked to investigate the appearance of a crop circle."

"Aliens," said Ryan, perking up.

"There's no such thing. It's just kids causing trouble."

"But you don't know that," Ryan countered. "Actually, while some people do still think they are caused by aliens, the new age belief is that they are linked to ancient energy and nature, and that they appear in areas near historic ley lines and stone circles."

Keya moaned, "I hope none appear near the Rollright Standing Stones before the summer solstice. I could do without more people being drawn to the area. Still, I suppose we better investigate."

CHAPTER SIX

On Friday evening, Dotty picked Keya up from her home in the small Cotswold village of Ampney St Martin, five miles to the east of Cirencester.

Dotty drove a smart metallic-grey Audi A1 and Keya half expected to find Dotty's large, fluffy grey cat on the back seat.

"How's Earl Grey?" Keya asked as she climbed into the passenger seat.

Dotty tucked a strand of her bobbed fair hair behind her ear as she replied, "He loves being back at Meadowbank Farm. As the weather's warmer, he spends most of his time outside, either searching for mice or keeping Agatha, Aunt Beanie's pig, company."

After over a year away, Dotty had returned to the Cotswolds and to Meadowbank Farm where Aunt Beanie lived. Ryan had moved into Dotty's farm cottage when she'd left, but he'd found himself similar lodgings at a farm in Stratton, a village to the north of Cirencester, which had been swallowed up by the expanding town.

"And are you settled back in the cottage?"

"Oh yes. Ryan's looked after everything well, although Aunt Beanie did mention that Monica came the Monday before I moved back in, and she probably gave the cottage a thorough clean."

"And how is your course?" Keya asked.

Dotty was taking a business course in Oxford as she prepared to set up her own antique emporium in a barn at Meadowbank Farm. Keya had thought Gilly would be annoyed, but she was actually delighted and said that another local antiques shop would only draw more people to the area.

Dotty had previously worked at Akemans, and learned her trade there, so Keya was relieved that her two friends wouldn't be falling out over the new business venture.

"I'm just doing the foundation course at the moment, and it's hard enough. Who knew there was so much to think about with your own business? Do you do your own accounts?" Dotty asked.

"No way. I have too much to do. But Zivah, and now Millie, always check the day's takings against the customer invoices, and we send everything to a company in Cheltenham who compiles our tax returns. They tell me we'll need to register for VAT soon, which is a pain. I can't charge customers more to cover it, but most of my supplies, being fresh food and ingredients, are zero rated, so we won't be able to offset their costs."

"You see, that is just the sort of thing I need to know," said Dotty, indicating right.

They drove along the Fosse Way, an old Roman road which cut straight across the Cotswolds.

By the time they arrived at Dover's Hill, to the west of Chipping Campden where the Olympick Games were being held, the National Trust's gravel car park was nearly full. Dotty managed to squeeze into a space, half on the gravel and half on a grassy bank.

"That was lucky," Dotty admitted. "Otherwise, we'd have had to find somewhere else to park and walk back."

"I noticed a sign for the Cotswold Way. Did you know Ryan and Millie are planning to run it?" Keya asked as she lifted a small rucksack onto her back, containing her waterproof coat, a water bottle, and snacks.

"No," Dotty replied, as they joined a steady stream of people making their way up the hill.

Keya spotted the Wimsey family and she and Dotty sat down with them on the edge of a grassy slope overlooking a roped-off area where two men were facing each other. Both were wearing white smocks, and gripping each other's shoulders, pushing back and forth, and frequently swinging out a foot and attempting to hit their opponent's shins.

"Ow!" Dotty exclaimed when one particularly vicious kick hit home.

Gilly's sixteen-year-old son, Thomas, clapped, but fourteen-year-old Olivia turned to Keya and Dotty, who were both sitting on their waterproof coats, and explained, "It doesn't really hurt. Their trousers are stuffed with straw."

Keya peered at the men's legs and realised that one man had stalks of golden straw poking out of his white socks, which were pulled up over the ends of his jeans. She found the whole thing rather bizarre.

"I thought Sujin might be with you," Gilly probed.

Sujin was the station's crime scene technician, and he and Keya were friends.

"No, he's playing at a pub in Stow-on-the-Wold tonight."

Dotty turned her head and said, "I didn't know that. Do you want to pop in on our way home?"

"Maybe," Keya mumbled.

She liked Sujin. Maybe more than just liked, but she didn't trust her feelings and, besides, she had far too much to do at the moment without getting into a romantic relationship. But then, she wasn't getting any younger …

"I heard his band, the Celtic Twisters, play recently," Dr Peter said. He pushed his black-framed glasses up his nose and added. "They're very good, and I was impressed by Sujin's fiddle playing. He's quite the dark horse."

At work, Sujin was quiet and unassuming, but he came to life when he played his fiddle, or electric violin, for the band, which played a mixture of Scottish and Irish music, folk songs, and ballads.

"It's nice to see you out enjoying yourself, Dr Peter," Dotty said. Keya felt her wince as another kick landed on one of the men's shins. A man in a white coat, presumably the referee, poked one of the men with his long stick and the men parted and stepped back. Then the contest began again.

"It's so freeing to have Erwin working with me. I don't know why I didn't look for an associate earlier," Dr Peter reflected.

Keya had met Erwin Carter when Gilly had seated them next to each other at a dinner party. Gilly didn't exactly admit she'd been trying to set them up, but both she and Keya knew she had.

"Because," Gilly said, "you didn't believe anyone could look after your patients as well as you can."

"Well, I'm not sure about that," mumbled Dr Peter, turning his attention back to the two men who tumbled to the ground.

Gilly rolled her eyes at Keya as the white-coated man walked towards the two men and blew a whistle.

Everyone, including Keya, clapped.

Next it was the turn of two women, both clad in white frocks and black leggings. Their legs looked too thin and uniform to have protective layers of straw, as the men had done.

"I've persuaded Aunt Beanie to come with me for the summer solstice at the standing stones. Do you want to join us?" Gilly asked.

"We're going to watch *A Midsummer Night's Dream* at the Rococo Gardens, aren't we, Dotty?" Keya replied.

"Yes," Dotty answered, inattentively. "Oh, why would you want to do this?" she asked, watching the two women attack each other's legs.

"That sounds far more pleasant than sitting around in the cold and dark waiting for the sun to rise," Dr Peter remarked.

"They are planning to have a small fire this year," Keya remembered.

"See, Peter. It'll be a lovely night and I know it'll help me feel closer to my Celtic ancestors."

This time, Dr Peter rolled his eyes.

CHAPTER SEVEN

On Tuesday 20th June, the eve of the midsummer solstice, Keya arrived back at Cirencester Police Station in the mid-afternoon.

"Arrest any aliens?" Stan asked as he followed her into the team room, but then he asked more helpfully, "Would you like a cuppa?"

Keya replied, "Yes, please, and I thought we'd established that it's not aliens making the crop circles but the ancients sending us a message. And as we're approaching the summer solstice, they seem to have a lot to say. Like please visit our village and spend money at the local shops and pub."

"Do you think this is just a publicity stunt?" Ryan asked innocently.

"What else do you put it down to? It's not the work of aliens or an ancient mystical force, whatever people want to believe."

"And I doubt it's Doug and Dave."

"Who are they?" asked Keya.

"Aren't they singers?" Ryan queried.

Stan regarded Ryan steadily. "No, that's Chaz and Dave. Doug and Dave were two pranksters from Southampton who fooled the world during the 1980s by creating over two hundred crop circles. They tied ropes to planks of wood and used them to stamp out their designs."

"But I don't see how they could have created the one I visited today at Asthall Leigh. It was intricate and, from the drone image one of the locals produced, completely symmetrical. How could two blokes with oversized pieces of wood on their feet create that?" Keya demanded.

"Such is the conundrum of crop circles," Stan commented as he left the room.

Keya sat down and looked across at Ryan, whose brow wrinkled as he regarded her.

"You're not worried about this outbreak of crop circles, are you?" she asked him.

"No, but I am concerned about the play this evening. What if I don't understand what's going on?"

"Then you won't be the only one. I never could get my head round Shakespeare."

"What's *A Midsummer Night's Dream* about? Millie says it's a comedy, but what if I don't find it funny?"

"Let's see what we can find out about it. Someone must have posted a summary online." Keya switched her computer on as Stan reappeared carrying two cups. He placed her tea on her desk as she typed in 'what is midsummer night's dream about?'.

There were plenty of Shakespeare related results. She clicked on the first one. Then she looked up at Ryan and read, "The play is a comedy and it's set in a court in ancient Athens, and a mystical forest outside the city walls. It covers the themes of love, magic, dreams, and mischief."

"I like the mischief part," said Ryan.

"Are you going to Painswick tonight, to the open-air theatre?" Stan asked.

"Yes, but we want to make sure we know what's going on," Keya confessed as she turned her attention back to the computer screen.

"*A Midsummer Night's Dream* is one of Shakespeare's lighter plays," Stan declared, and Keya and Ryan looked up at him in surprise.

"I watched it last year," he admitted, before going on to outline the entire plot.

When he finished, Ryan said uncertainly, "It doesn't sound particularly funny,"

"That's in the acting," Stan reassured him.

"I'm grateful for the explanation. Thanks, Stan," Keya said.

"You're welcome, and I hope you enjoy it. I understand that tonight is special, and there'll be acrobats and circus performers and a light show during the interval."

"Now that does sound interesting," Ryan perked up.

Keya and Ryan both left the station at five o'clock.

"Dotty's picking me up tonight. Are we meeting you there?" asked Keya.

"Yes, I'm collecting Millie from the cafe with part of the picnic which she and Dotty have organised."

Keya looked up at the still blue sky and said, "I'm actually starting to look forward to tonight. A relaxed evening out with friends."

CHAPTER EIGHT

Keya clapped her hands along with the rest of the crowd, who'd enjoyed the first half of the outdoor performance of *A Midsummer Night's Dream*.

A temporary stage had been erected in front of a beech wood, which added to the setting of the magical forest. The audience were sitting on a variety of picnic blankets and camping chairs in a field in front of the grand, but not too large, Painswick House.

"Are there any sausage rolls left?" Ryan asked.

"No, you ate the last one," giggled Millie.

She and Ryan half lay, half sat on a red and white checked picnic blanket, with most of the remains of the picnic scattered round Ryan.

Behind them, facing the stage, Keya and Dotty occupied two folding blue camping chairs Dotty had borrowed from Aunt Beanie.

"I actually understood most of that," Keya remarked, "although I doubt I would have done if Stan hadn't given me a rundown."

"Would anyone like to look round the garden trail before the second half?" asked Dotty tentatively.

"Oh yes," Ryan replied, sitting up.

"We better tidy up the picnic first," Millie suggested.

"But don't pack these sandwiches away. I might feel peckish in the second half." Ryan pressed down the lid on a plastic container containing an assortment of filled rolls.

"I'm sure you will." Millie smiled at him indulgently.

They all helped gather up the picnic items. Dotty and Millie had provided an excellent spread and Keya had particularly enjoyed their mini spinach, leek, and goat's cheese tarts.

When they'd finished, they followed other members of the audience through a narrow wooden gate into the beech wood. It had seemed relatively light out in the field, but in the wood it felt far darker. Long strings of lights hung from the branches of beech trees and illuminated a wood chip path.

Suddenly, Keya saw a blast of fire up ahead. She quickened her pace, but as she drew closer, she realised it was only a fire-eating act.

When Dotty caught up, she said, "I don't know how she does that." They watched as a woman wearing a red leotard with black fishnet tights swallowed the flaming end of a metal torch. "I'm sorry Sujin couldn't come tonight."

"He'd have enjoyed this, but he also loves playing in his band. And tonight they're performing at a mini festival. They and several other bands are playing through the night and welcoming in the summer solstice," Keya explained.

"That sounds both exciting and exhausting," considered Dotty. She stared as the fire-eater juggled three flaming torches before asking, "Do you think you two will ever be more than just good friends?"

"Will you and Zach?" Keya countered. They walked down a woodland path. A beam of soft blue light illuminated the carving of an owl perched on a tree branch.

"I'm not sure. I think I'd like to. Zach is considerate, intelligent …"

"And tall, dark, and handsome. I've seen the photos of you with him in Northumberland," interjected Keya.

"Yes, that as well."

Keya thought her friend was blushing.

"But he's wrapped up in his family history research. And then there's his old flame back in the US. I'm not sure where I stand. It's up to him."

"That doesn't sound particularly reasonable or satisfactory. Are you just going to hang around while he makes up his mind?"

"No," Dotty said decisively as the path between the beech trees climbed steadily. Beams of coloured light moved around, illuminating carvings and large ornaments hanging from tree branches. It was like the enchanted forest depicted in the play.

Dotty continued, "Which is why I've returned to the Cotswolds and I'm taking this business course before setting up my own antique shop. My mum is right. I can't put my life on hold for him. I have to get on with it."

"And you might find someone else," Keya suggested in an upbeat voice.

"Exactly," Dotty replied, although she didn't sound convinced. For the second time she asked, "And what about you and Sujin?"

The path led them out of the wood to a lone tree from which an acrobat was suspended. They watched as she slowly turned a circle and extended her legs skyward.

Keya considered and then replied, "You know when you get on really well with someone, especially a work colleague, and you don't want to ruin it?"

"Yes, I know what you mean," Dotty responded.

"Well that's how I feel at the moment. I don't want to mess up a great friendship."

"But are you satisfied with that?" Dotty asked as they reached a stone-flagged pool. The water was illuminated, and a young woman wearing a mermaid's costume was lying on the steps, her tail flapping in the water.

"Generally. Although sometimes I'd like there to be more. But what difference would it make? He has his band, so even on the few occasions I have the time and energy to go out, he's busy. Besides, I have you to expand my cultural awareness!"

Keya linked her arm through Dotty's, and they continued up the path to the top of the formal garden. A crowd of people were watching three acrobats perform in front of a white curved screen with arches and ornamental battlements.

Keya thought gratefully that at least she had her friends, and that was all she needed on a balmy summer night on the eve of the summer solstice.

CHAPTER NINE

Groggily, Keya thought she could hear her phone ringing.
Who could be calling? What time was it?

It had been well after midnight when she'd climbed into bed, and although she'd been tired, her brain must have been processing the evening's performance as she'd slept fitfully.

Yes, that was her phone.

Reaching out her hand, she fumbled to find it and as she did, she propped herself up on one elbow and answered sleepily, "Hello."

"Keya, it's Gilly. There's a body."

Was this a joke?

"What body?"

"At the standing stones. A young woman called Daisy Bentham."

"Daisy!" Keya exclaimed, sitting up. She realised it wasn't that dark and sunlight was penetrating her bright tropical-themed curtains with their pink flamingo design.

Surely not Daisy from the bakery.

"Do you know her?" asked Gilly uncertainly.

"She might be the Daisy who baked the bread we tried last week. Where are you?"

"Knights Farm Shop. Aunt Beanie sent me. She was trying to take charge at the standing stones, but it was rather chaotic."

"It's going to take me nearly an hour to get to you. Can you stop people leaving?"

"Too late. Finding a dead body rather dampened the celebratory mood and people started walking out as soon as it was discovered. Aunt Beanie instructed me to take photos, but I had to be careful after a man with dreadlocks threatened to smash my phone when I tried to snap a picture of him. And my battery's running low, so please hurry."

Keya jumped out of bed and fell over her shoes.

"Oh Toda!" she exclaimed. It was a phrase she turned to when trying not to swear.

Pushing herself to her feet, and rubbing her knees, she remembered the phrase 'more haste, less speed'.

She decided she needed a shower to wake herself up. After that, dressed in her police uniform, she made herself a cup of coffee in a Waterwheel branded thermal mug, grabbed her crime scene bag, and headed out of the front door.

As she hurried down the garden path, she heard her neighbour and landlady, Peggy, call, "Trouble already?"

Keya turned and looked up at the window of the plain-fronted brick house which adjoined hers.

"I'm afraid so. Somebody's found a body up at the standing stones." Keya realised she shouldn't have told Peggy that, but as she switched on the engine of her marine-blue Polo, because her official police vehicle was at the station, the car radio came to life.

It was tuned into the local Corinium Radio station, and the news headlines opened with the disturbing story of the body of a young woman at the Rollright standing stones. The report added that it had been discovered as the sun rose over the Cotswolds on the summer solstice.

So much for keeping the death quiet. The local press was likely to arrive before she did. She called Ryan.

"I've just heard the news," he said, answering her call immediately. "Is this our case?"

"Unless someone else gets there before me. Gilly called and I'm on my way, but it'll take me half an hour. In the meantime, Aunt Beanie is in charge."

"Is that good or bad?" Ryan asked.

"I've no idea."

Keya's next call was to her boss, Inspector Evans.

He sounded as if her call had woken him, but he listened to her explanation before he said, "Very well, Sergeant. Keep me informed. I'll sort out the coroner and the forensics side." Despite his mother's death, the inspector continued to work in the same professional, but sometimes unorthodox manner he always had, and he seemed to thrive when complex or important cases turned up.

Finishing the call, Keya realised the inspector was right and that the person they most needed at the scene, if there really was a dead body, was Sujin, their crime scene technician. She wondered if he was still at the mini festival or if he'd just climbed into bed and the inspector's call would wake him.

Keya slowed as she approached the area of the standing stones. Cars were parked on the verges as well as in the lay-bys. So much for Daisy receiving permission from the farm shop for everyone to park there. On the road, groups of people were hanging about, apparently waiting for something to happen.

Keya parked behind the first car she came to. Removing a blue 'Police Slow' sign from the back of her car, she positioned it in the road. She carried another one with her, along with a bag of crime scene essentials, and walked towards the coppice and the entrance to the grassy area where the standing stones were.

"There you are!" cried Gilly, rushing towards Keya.

All eyes turned to stare at the two of them.

"What took you so long?" remonstrated Gilly.

Keya ignored the question and asked, "What's the situation?"

"Aunt Beanie took charge until a Dr Reid turned up and told her he was taking over. I thought Aunt Beanie was about to argue, but she looked down at the body of the dead woman and the boyfriend who was refusing to leave her side and changed her mind. She's consoling the boyfriend now, and she sent me back out to wait for you. And here you are."

"Here I am," Keya confirmed. "And the first thing I need to do is prevent another accident. Can you carry this sign to the far end of the parked cars and position it behind them? This road gets busy, and we need to slow the traffic down. And I should move these people on. We can't have them loitering around by the side of the road."

"I don't think there's much you can do about them on your own," Gilly replied. "I did suggest to some of them that they wait at the farm shop, but they just ignored me."

Conscious that she was the focus of everyone's attention, Keya left the sign with Gilly and entered the small coppice where more people were sitting on stone benches or beside them on the grass.

She expected to find crowds of people milling in and around the standing stones, so she was surprised to find a rope cordoning off the area. One end was attached to the fence surrounding the coppice and the other to a branch which had been driven into the ground halfway towards another small wood.

Beyond the cordon, forty or so people were sitting quietly inside the stone circle. In the centre, a woman wearing a shawl, who Keya thought might be Aurora, placed a piece of wood on a fire. Keya sniffed and watched the wisps of smoke hanging in the air.

In the far corner, a woman waved energetically. It was Aunt Beanie, although the bow of her bright yellow headscarf appeared to have wilted on top of her head. Sitting on a camp chair beside her was a slumped figure whose face was hidden in their hands.

As Keya searched for the body, another figure lifted his hat in acknowledgement. It was Dr Reid. She approached him as he stood on the far side of the nearest standing stones.

"This is quite terrible. I knew nothing good would come of the summer solstice gathering, but a dead body? And Daisy, of all people."

Keya struggled to swallow and felt a pain at the back of her throat. It was the Daisy she'd met. But who'd want to hurt such a sweet young woman? A woman so full of life. Keya gulped. Not any longer. And she was jumping to conclusions.

"Do you know how she died, doctor?"

"No. But then I'm not a medical doctor. My specialty is archaeology and ancient history."

He cleared his throat and continued, "But there's nothing obvious, like a wound or blood. In fact, she looks very peaceful resting against the stone. You do hear of young people having heart attacks, don't you?"

"Yes," Keya confirmed. "It does happen." But to Daisy? she thought. "Can you show me the body?"

Again, Keya felt all eyes trained on her as she stepped inside the stone circle. She shivered as she felt a cold, unpleasant sensation, despite the warmth of the fire and the sun climbing in the sky.

She turned to face the stones, and there, sitting down but slumped against one of the stones, was the pale figure of Daisy.

CHAPTER TEN

Daisy did look peaceful as she leaned against the irregular and pitted stone which was covered in shades of green lichen. Her waist-length hair was spread over her shoulders and the blonde streaks caught the early morning rays of sunshine. A crown of wildflowers was resting on her head.

Using the end of her pen, Keya gently lifted the home-made circle of flowers, but she didn't see any blood beneath it.

As the non-medical Dr Reid had said, there was no apparent cause of death.

Keya straightened up and realised that the crowd of people beyond the makeshift cordon was swelling, which hopefully meant fewer people on the roadside. But she didn't want them coming any closer to the crime scene. If indeed a crime had been committed. At the moment, that was far from clear.

But Daisy's passing was certainly suspicious, and investigating such deaths was part of her role as a police officer.

Watching the crowd press forward, she asked, "Who put up the cordon, Dr Reid?"

"I did, with Dora's help."

Keya hadn't seen the thin, grey-haired Dora, but Dr Reid raised his hat again and she appeared from further round the stone circle.

Keya removed a roll of white tape with 'police' stamped on it in blue letters.

She handed it to Dr Reid, who said, "Dora, I believe Sergeant Varma would like us to make the cordon official. Isn't that right, Sergeant?"

"Yes, and longer. From the fence beside the entrance to the one surrounding the wood on the edge of the field, please."

"What about Daisy?" Dora implored.

"Leave the police to deal with her," Dr Reid responded, in a tone which implied it was none of Dora's business.

Dora paled to such an extent the colour of her face matched her hair.

Concerned, Keya responded, "I have to wait for the coroner and the crime scene technician to arrive." Then she added, "But she'll come to no harm sitting out in the sunshine."

This seemed to satisfy Dora.

As Dr Reid and Dora moved towards the crowd, there was a shout from the edge of it, and a parting of bodies.

"Daisy. Where's my Daisy?" cried a middle-aged woman wearing a pair of faded jeans, a pale blue T-shirt and a thin white nylon cardigan.

Dr Reid attempted to intercept her as he called loudly, "Doreen."

Ignoring him, the woman's gaze latched onto Keya, and she hurried towards her.

Keya stepped out of the stone circle and immediately felt lighter, with a clearer head. Soft sunshine warmed her face.

"Can I help you, Mrs…?" Keya asked the approaching woman.

"Skinner. Mrs Skinner, but where is my Daisy?"

"Daisy Bentham?" Keya clarified.

"Yes, she's my daughter and there's a terrible rumour in the village that she's …"

Mrs Skinner couldn't bring herself to finish the sentence as she wrung her hands together.

"I really am very sorry, Mrs Skinner, but I'm afraid Daisy has passed away." Keya wasn't sure why she used such an old-fashioned phrase, but it seemed a gentler one to use for this grieving mother.

But it didn't seem to help.

"Where? Where is she?" Mrs Skinner pushed past Keya, stepped into the stone circle, and turned towards her dead daughter.

As Keya followed quickly, Daisy's mother slumped to her knees and cried, "No, Daisy. It can't be. There must be some mistake. Not you. You can't be dead."

Keya gently, but firmly, pulled the distraught woman to her feet and said in a sympathetic tone, "I'm afraid she is."

Mrs Skinner attempted to break away, but Keya gripped her arm more firmly and added, "And until we establish how she died, we mustn't disturb her." These were the most delicate words Keya could think of to describe the crime scene.

There was a muttering in the crowd and disgruntled voices as people parted to allow Gilly Wimsey through. As she ducked under the newly assembled police tape cordon, Dr Reid said authoritatively, "Stay back, this is a crime scene."

"I know," Gilly retorted, red-faced. "I'm the one who called the police."

When Gilly reached Keya, she exclaimed, "I had to keep moving the sign. There are more cars coming rather than less, and watch out, one of those outdoor broadcasting lorries has turned up."

Oh no, Keya thought. She'd soon have the press to deal with on top of everything else.

"Gilly, this is Mrs Skinner, Daisy, our dead girl's mother. She's understandably upset, but I need to …"

"Come with me, Mrs Skinner. I think we have some tea left in one of our flasks."

"Please, call me Doreen."

Doreen glanced back at Daisy before allowing Gilly to lead her away.

"Excuse me. Police. Please let us through," Ryan nearly shouted, his frustration audible.

Keya watched his black police hat bob up and down and then he emerged from the crowd, carrying a black bag, and making room for the smaller figure of Sujin, who was wearing a protective white forensic suit. He was carrying another bag and pulling a black canvas case.

Reaching Keya, Ryan told her, "I've called the inspector and requested backup to deal with the crowd. And with the reporters. Someone poked a microphone in my face as I was helping Sujin get his stuff through the entrance gate."

Ryan stopped for breath and looked at Keya. "Sorry. But it's rather a circus out there." He looked round the standing stones and breathed in. "But at least you have everything under control here."

"That's the locals, not me." She glanced across at Dora and Dr Reid, who were securing the end of the police tape to an intact section of wooden fencing around the small wood at the side of the field.

"I can see it's too late to ask you to put on a protective suit, Keya, but can you and Ryan at least cover your shoes?" Sujin held up some blue plastic shoe covers.

As Keya pulled them on, she watched Sujin open his canvas case. He removed a thin cylindrical object and then approached Daisy's body. It was a torch, and he shone a beam of light into each eye before taking hold of her right wrist.

Returning to his canvas case, he said, "In the absence of a medical doctor, I can confirm our victim is deceased."

"But not how?" asked Keya.

"No. The coroner's office is on their way to collect her body, but perhaps you and Ryan can give me some space so I can try to find out."

Keya was impressed. Despite having no sleep, or very little, Sujin was professional and business-like.

She nodded and said, "And we should start taking witness statements."

CHAPTER ELEVEN

As soon as Keya and Ryan moved away from the standing stone against which Daisy's body was slumped, they were accosted by Aurora.

"Can we go now?" Aurora pleaded. She and her skinny black-haired friend, who hovered by her side, were both wearing blue tops with large yellow sunflowers printed on them. They had tasselled shawls round their shoulders and were both carrying wilted sunflowers. A rainbow-coloured bag was hanging from Aurora's arm.

"We have to open the shop. And after this," she swept her hand dramatically in front of her, "we're going to be busy." She didn't quite manage to hide the note of excitement in her voice.

"We need to speak to everyone," Keya replied, "but do you both live in the village?"

The two women nodded their heads.

"Then give your contact details to my colleague, Constable Ryan, and I'll interview you both later."

"So we can go?" Aurora asked hopefully.

Keya pulled at her chin. "Are you walking?"

"Yes, it's much easier going back down to the village."

"OK. After you've provided your contact details, and as long as you do so quietly." She emphasised the last word. "I don't want everyone rushing off before we've spoken to them."

But glancing around the stones, Keya thought those who'd wanted to leave already had, and everyone else looked settled and seemed to be savouring the scene playing out before them.

Keya and Ryan made their way slowly around the ring of stones, speaking to the people sitting quietly inside them. Keya discovered they'd come from all over the country. A lady called Deb, and her friend Liz, had travelled down from Durham. They told her they used to visit Stonehenge, but it was too busy now and they preferred the more relaxed atmosphere at the Rollright Standing Stones.

A woman called Bethany, who was accompanied by her sister, had even brought her seven-month-old baby boy with her. Keya marvelled as he slept peacefully in the fabric carrier strapped to his mother's front.

At the far end of the stone circle, by the largest misshaped stone, was Aunt Beanie. Gilly and Doreen were sitting on a blue and green checked picnic blanket and a young man with dark-blonde hair was slumped in a green camping chair.

Aunt Beanie approached Keya and said, "I don't think you should speak to Theo near Doreen. She was very upset when she saw him, and I think she blames him for her daughter's death."

Keya glanced over at the small party beside the large stone.

"Can I come back to you? I want to make sure we speak to everyone who was here overnight, not that they have much to say. Nobody witnessed Daisy arguing with anyone, nor did she seem upset, worried, or angry. Everyone says she joined in the merriment until, feeling tired, she retired to sit down by the stone."

"And once it was dark, we only saw shadows and inconspicuous movements. Nobody appeared concerned about Daisy, and it was only after sunrise and when the celebrations had started that anyone realised Theo was panicking because he couldn't wake Daisy."

Aunt Beanie glanced across at the slumped man and added, "That's when I went over to try to help. But as soon as I touched Daisy, I knew she was dead."

There was muttering in the crowd, and Keya and Aunt Beanie

watched as the brown- suited figure of Inspector Evans pushed his way through. His rugby player build came in handy on these occasions. He was followed by three uniformed police officers who Keya recognised but didn't know personally.

Inspector Evans spoke to the officers, who approached members of the crowd, notepads and pens at the ready.

"I better brief the inspector," Keya said. She strode across the centre of the stone circle, skirting the glowing embers of the fire, and stepped out to meet her boss. Once again, she felt an almost palpable relief at being outside the ring of stone.

"Having yourselves quite a party?" Inspector Evans commented. "But at least you erected a cordon."

"Actually, that was Dr Reid, chairman of the heritage committee, and Dora, the committee's secretary. But a lot of people have trampled around the crime scene, and some left before I got here," Keya replied.

"Is it a crime?" asked the inspector.

"We're not sure. Sujin is examining the body in situ." And then Keya went on to explain who the victim was, and what she'd found out since she'd arrived. "And Constable Ryan is still taking statements."

Keya watched Ryan as he spoke to a woman whose burgundy-coloured hair matched her coat.

"I'll speak to Sujin first," said the inspector, and he entered the stone circle. Reluctantly, Keya followed him.

Sujin had tipped the body forward and was examining Daisy's back.

Keya and Inspector Evans waited.

After Sujin respectfully settled the body against the rough rock, he looked up and said, "I can't tell you much, sir. And I haven't been able to discover if she was deliberately killed, if this was an accident, or if she died from natural causes. We'll have to wait for the results of the post-mortem."

They heard a female voice call, "Coming through," and two sage-green clad figures wheeled a stretcher towards Keya and the inspector.

"They're here to take the body away," Sujin said. He rocked back on his heels and added, "The evidence around the body is what you'd expect from an event like this. An empty crisp packet, an empty can of cider, and the end of a roll-up cigarette. I'll examine them, and whatever else I find, back at the station. But now I need to help move the body." Sujin stood up and raised his hand, which the lead ambulance worker acknowledged with a nod of her head.

Inspector Evans stepped away, towards the dying fire, and Keya followed him. Lowering his voice, the inspector asked, "Next of kin?"

"A mother. I don't think she was here overnight, but when she saw the body, she became rather distressed. Gilly Wimsey is trying to comfort her. And the man in the chair near Aunt Beanie is the dead woman's boyfriend. He was with her last night. They share a house in the village, and he runs the local mill."

"Sir Anthony's nephew?" enquired the inspector.

"I believe so," Keya replied, wondering how the inspector knew the mill owner.

"And is there a father?"

"I don't know, sir. Let me try to find out."

"And while you do, I'll speak to Constable Ryan."

Keya and the inspector separated and Keya rejoined Aunt Beanie. "The inspector wonders if there is anyone else we need to inform about Daisy's death?"

Aunt Beanie replied, "I heard Theo mutter about a father and a sister who I think live in the village. Do you know how much longer we'll be?"

"I'm not sure."

Keya returned to Ryan and Inspector Evans and said, "We think there's a father and a sister living in the village. Would you like me to speak to them?"

"Yes, although they'll probably already know about the death. Village gossip is more effective than any social media channel. But see how they are and what they know. If they're too upset, contact Inspector Sue and see if she can act as our family liaison officer. In fact, I'll call her myself and ask her to come over. We might need her help with the mother."

"And Theo, the boyfriend?" Keya asked.

"Constable Jenkins can escort him back to the station, and can you ask Bernadette," -which was Aunt Beanie's formal name - "and Gilly Wimsey to join us there?"

"Can they go home to shower and change first?"

"Yes. Ask them to come to the station at two o'clock. That should give us enough time to speak to everyone we need to here, and in Lower Rollright."

CHAPTER TWELVE

Inspector Evans changed his mind and tasked another officer to accompany Theo to Cirencester Police Station. He sent Ryan with Keya, in her little blue Polo, to find Daisy's father and sister.

Ryan pushed the passenger seat as far back as it would go and folded himself into it.

Dr Reid, who'd attached himself to Inspector Evans once he'd realised he was the lead officer, had told Keya that Daisy's father and teenage sister lived on Barley Row, and to find it she should take the first turning on the left, up the hill, after the pub.

"Surely they'll already know about the death," Ryan said as Keya drove into Lower Rollright.

"I expect so, but some people actively avoid listening to or reading the news. And I can't say I blame them. It's usually depressing," Keya replied.

Number 3 Barley Row was one of a line of five small, stone, terraced cottages. Unlike the others, there were no containers of flowers or hanging baskets outside. Just a worn and ripped mat that had probably once had 'Welcome' printed on it.

Keya used a metal door knocker to announce their presence.

They waited several minutes, and Keya was considering trying the door handle or peering through a grimy window, when the door opened and a dishevelled, unshaven, plump man looked out. He was still wearing a pair of checked cotton pyjama bottoms and a stained white sleeveless vest, even though it was now mid-morning.

"I was wondering when you lot would turn up."

"Mr Skinner?" Keya asked.

"Skinner," spat the man. "That was the bounder my wife ran off with. It's Bentham. Dennis Bentham, and you better come in. Walls have ears, but doorsteps also have prying eyes."

Ryan ducked as he entered the cottage, and they found themselves in a cramped living room. It was a state. Empty beer cans, together with used plates, glasses and mugs, littered the coffee and side tables, and shoes and articles of crumpled clothing covered the floor.

The air hung heavy with the smell of burnt fat.

"Sit down, if you can find a space. Things have gone to pot since Doreen ran away and Daisy left us. And Zoe's not much use. When she's not at school, she's being fed rubbish by Aurora and her friend, Viv. They were the ones who told us about Daisy, and they took Zoe with them. You'll probably find her at their shop."

Keya and Ryan had both remained standing. Keya asked, "So you know about your daughter's death?"

"I know she's dead. Aurora couldn't quite hide her excitement at breaking the news to me, but she couldn't tell me how Daisy died. Was it an accident?"

"I'm afraid we don't know the precise circumstances at the moment, sir," Keya replied formally.

"Please, call me Dennis. I believe in plain speaking and not standing on ceremony. So you'll have to …"

Dennis stopped, and his face turned ashen. He collapsed onto the sofa, sitting on top of a black jacket.

Keya thought he'd been about to say 'cut her up' and could understand why Dennis hadn't been able to continue. So she said, "Her body will be examined by a pathologist to ascertain the cause of death."

"Daisy, my poor little girl," whimpered a forlorn Dennis.

Keya suspected they wouldn't get anything else of use out of Dennis Bentham for the moment, so she said, "I'll ask the family liaison officer to visit, but is there anyone you'd like to come over and be with you?"

Dennis slowly shook his head.

Politely, and because they was the obligatory words for such an occasion, Keya uttered, "Sorry for your loss," before she and Ryan left the cottage.

Outside, Keya breathed in lungfuls of fresh air.

"How can he live like that?" Ryan asked.

"He probably doesn't notice. And if he's always been used to someone else clearing up after him …" Keya's voice trailed off. She shrugged her shoulders and suggested, "Let's find Zoe."

Leaving Keya's car parked on Barley Row, they walked down the narrow lane. At the bottom, where it joined the road on which the pub and Daisy's bakery were located, Keya noticed a wooden sign with 'Footpath to the Standing Stones' painted on it. It was pointing up Barley Row.

Keya and Ryan entered Aurora's purple-fronted shop and found they weren't the only visitors.

"Officers," called Aurora imperiously over the chatter. "What news?"

All conversation ceased immediately.

"Um," Keya hesitated. Then taking hold of herself, she ignored the onlookers and said to Aurora, "We'd like to speak to Zoe."

"Daisy's sister is in the back. Viv is reading her palm," Aurora announced to the entire shop.

Ryan rolled his eyes.

Keya and Ryan pushed aside the hanging beads as they followed Aurora into a small space at the back of the shop. There was a soft, delicate smell of lavender.

The only light came from a candle on a central circular table. Viv was holding the hand of a girl whose back was to Ryan and Keya. She had long, brown hair, which was neatly trimmed and stopped just below her shoulders.

Viv ignored them as she said in a sincere voice. "The pain will dissipate and then you will find love."

The girl must have sensed their presence, as she pulled her hand away and turned to look at the new arrivals. Even in the poor light,

Keya could see her eyes were red and puffy and it was clear she'd been crying.

"Zoe Bentham?" Keya asked in a gentle voice.

"Yes," sniffed the girl. Keya realised she could only be sixteen or seventeen and was probably supposed to be at school today. What if she was missing her exams? A levels were held in June.

"I'm Sergeant Varma, and this is my colleague, Constable Jenkins. We'd like to speak to you about your sister. In private," Keya added, looking from Viv to Aurora.

"She's only seventeen," Aurora protested. "One of us should stay with her."

"I'll be OK," Zoe insisted. "There isn't anything you can do. I killed my sister!"

CHAPTER THIRTEEN

Aurora gasped, and Viv reached out and touched Zoe's arm. "Why did you say that? You weren't even up at the standing stones."

Keya decided she'd had enough of the dimly lit room and, spotting a thick blackout blind on the side wall, she crossed to it and pulled the cord. Sunlight filled the room.

"That's better," she said. "Now, Zoe. Why do you think you had something to do with your sister's death?"

"She wouldn't come home. I begged and begged her to. You have no idea what it's like living on my own with Dad," sobbed Zoe.

Keya could imagine. Zoe's slovenly father probably expected her to keep home for him as if she was his wife, not a young woman with studies and plans for her own life.

"It was bad enough when Mum left. I was so angry with her, but I think I understand now. I wouldn't want to be married to Dad. But Daisy could manage him. She's always been his favourite. She wrote up lists of chores and made sure we did them, even Dad. And she took on the bulk of the work herself. But then she and Dad had a huge row about Theo, and he kicked her out. I thought she'd soon be back, but she likes living with Theo. She has a lovely garden. And then she opened the bakery, and …"

Zoe sobbed loudly. "And forgot about me."

Aurora pulled up a stool and sat down beside Zoe, placing a protective arm around her. She murmured in a sincere tone, "I'm sure she didn't. I know she put aside bread and cakes and had Ash deliver them to you and your dad. And she always waved when she drove or walked past and saw you in the shop."

Zoe looked into Aurora's eyes and said, "But she didn't come home. Even when I begged her to. Which is why I asked the midsummer fairies to make her. But she must have refused them, too. And they placed a spell on her. And she won't wake up."

Aurora looked up at Keya, and there were tears in her eyes.

To Keya's surprise, it was Ryan who spoke next.

"It wasn't the fairies, Zoe. If they make mistakes, or play tricks on people, they always make them right. But Daisy didn't wake up."

"I know, Aurora and Viv told me. But how can you be sure it wasn't the fairies?"

Ryan answered again. "Because they want Midsummer's Day to be a time of celebration. They wouldn't have left Daisy asleep. I'm afraid something else happened to your sister and we're trying to find out what it was."

"Then it wasn't me?" Zoe looked like a young girl as she leaned into Aurora and rested her head on her front.

"No, Zoe," Keya reassured her. "It wasn't you. But when did you last see your sister?"

Zoe sniffed, and Aurora loosened her grip. "What we all need is a cup of tea. And Viv, you should check the shop. Who knows what's been taken while we've been in here? Will you be all right, pet?" Aurora asked Zoe.

Zoe nodded, so Viv left the room, followed through the jangling beads by Aurora.

Then Zoe explained, "On Sunday, I went to her and Theo's house for lunch. She made nachos and fajitas. They're my favourite. Dad won't eat anything foreign. He's strictly meat and potatoes."

"And how did your sister seem?"

"She was happy, and very excited about the summer solstice event up at the stones. Theo protested and said he couldn't go because he needed to prepare the mill for the incoming harvest. But Daisy pleaded with him, and of course, he agreed to go with her."

"Did you want to go too?"

"I did, but Dad wouldn't let me, and I'm supposed to be at school today."

"Do you have an exam?" Keya asked in a concerned tone.

"No, my A levels are next year."

"And you didn't see Daisy yesterday or Monday?" Keya pressed.

"No, I was at school both days and yesterday I helped Aurora and Viv in the shop after school while they got ready for the solstice event up at the stones. I did see Daisy leave the bakery on foot and she waved to me, but she didn't stop."

"What time was that?"

"Just after five o'clock, I think."

"And did she appear to be in a hurry?"

"Yes, but then she also had to get ready to go up to the standing stones."

"And she was on her own? You didn't see her stop and speak to anyone?" Keya asked.

"No, she just walked down the street and past the pub. And that was the last I saw of her."

The tears and the sobs started again.

Aurora backed into the small room carrying a tray of hourglass-shaped mugs in bold floral patterns and colours. Keya caught a much stronger aroma of lavender.

"Lavender tea," Aurora announced. "Good for relaxation and relieving stress and anxiety."

"It smells very aromatic, but I'm afraid we have to go," Keya said. "But I will need to come back and take statements from you and Viv." But not now, Keya thought. She really didn't fancy lavender tea.

Outside Aurora's shop, Keya once again breathed in lungfuls of fresh air. It really was a lovely summer day. Too nice to be working on such a tragic case.

Her stomach rumbled. It was way past breakfast time and all she'd had was an early morning coffee on her drive to the standing stones.

"I need something to eat," she told Ryan, who looked relieved.

They walked the few metres to the bakery, but the front door was closed.

"Let's try the shop on the main road," Keya suggested, and they turned round.

They walked past the solid stone building of the Malt Shovel pub, and then Keya heard the calming trickle of water. As they approached the stone bridge, she saw a shallow stream. Compared with the River Coln, which ran alongside her cafe, it didn't look large enough to have once powered the waterwheel for Lower Rollright's mill.

The Rollright Village Store was well stocked with an assortment of everyday items, as well as postcards and Standing Stones themed merchandise. It was much larger than it appeared from the outside, and the rear, windowless section was given over to books and a wall dedicated to the history of the standing stones.

Dora, wearing a pair of yellow rubber gloves passed Keya carrying a plastic bucket of foaming water. She said to the woman behind the counter, "I've had another go at the stain from last week. It's still a dull orange, but hopefully it'll fade."

"Ash had to drop that bottle," the woman replied.

Approaching the counter, Keya observed a shelf containing an interesting selection of local honey, homemade chutney, and a tall bottle with a bright orange label with Rollright Hot Sauce printed on it.

Beside the till, Ryan was staring at a counter of ready-made sandwiches and a few lifeless looking salads in plastic containers.

There was also a self-service coffee machine. Not ideal. But it would have to do. She took a paper cup, placed it under the coffee machine's spout and pressed the button for a latte. She didn't usually drink coffee at this time, but she didn't fancy the machine's version of tea, and besides, she needed the extra caffeine.

She also picked up a packet of uninspiring looking egg mayonnaise sandwiches in plain white bread and, as a treat, a bar of chocolate.

As she approached the counter, a woman with a round face and short grey hair with blue undertones spotted her and enquired, with a note of reverence, "Are you investigating Daisy's death?"

"We are," Keya replied. "Did you know Daisy well?"

"Ever since we moved to the village fifteen years ago. Silas loves all things old, and he was drawn here by the standing stones. Daisy was just a girl back then, and the family seemed ... happy enough."

"When did Daisy's mother leave?"

"It must have been five years ago, maybe six. And it was quite a shock. To run off with another man and leave her children ... but I'm not sure I can blame her. Dennis isn't a pleasant man, especially with a drink inside him."

"Daisy's father, Dennis Bentham, has a problem with alcohol?"

"Oh, I wouldn't go as far as that, but he does spend a considerable amount of time in the Malt Shovel. And people say he's liable to raise his voice, if not his hand, when he gets home. I think Daisy could manage him, but her poor sister can't. I've considered calling social services, but I don't like to interfere," the woman said as she ran Keya's purchases across the till. "That'll be £7.89."

Keya handed over a £10 note and said, "Mrs ?"

"Reid. Silas is my husband."

Keya presumed she meant Dr Reid. "Mrs Reid, when did you last see Daisy?"

"I saw her van pass yesterday, but in person? Probably last week when I popped into the bakery to buy a loaf of her stoneground bread. It's so much nicer than the sliced stuff."

It was, Keya thought, picking up her sliced bread sandwiches and thinking of the far more appetising sandwich Daisy had made for her the week before.

"And did Daisy have any enemies in the village?"

"Enemies?" questioned Mrs Reid. "Everyone loved Daisy."

CHAPTER FOURTEEN

It was nearly midday by the time Keya and Ryan arrived at Cirencester Police Station. Keya's egg mayonnaise sandwich had been as disappointing as it looked, but the chocolate bar she'd eaten afterwards had almost made up for it.

She still felt alert, but that might have been from the caffeine in her latte. What she really wanted was a cup of normal tea, so she was relieved when Stan followed her into the team room and placed a mug on her desk.

"Thanks, that's exactly what I need. It's been a long morning already. Is the inspector interviewing Theo, the dead girl's boyfriend?"

"No. A lawyer arrived soon after Constable Sparrow brought him in, and they've been in discussions ever since. And so have the inspector and Chief Inspector Greg."

Keya sat down at her desk and turned on her computer. She found the case file Inspector Evans had opened and started writing up her notes from the morning. She found it a therapeutic exercise which, with the aid of her cup of tea, helped her process all that she'd seen and heard.

While there had been a lot of people up at the standing stones, they'd all said the same thing. Daisy had appeared happy, even joyful, and had laughed and danced next to the fire while someone played the flute, but as it started to grow dark, she'd complained that she felt tired, and Theo had helped her sit down beside one of the stones.

Someone thought they saw her smoking, but whether it was a cigarette or drugs, they weren't sure, and several people witnessed her drinking from a can.

As Aunt Beanie had said, it had been hard to tell what was happening once it grew dark, as the main light came from the fire and the glow sticks some of the revellers had been carrying.

Nobody had remembered seeing Daisy until it had started to get light. As the sun rose, a few people had spotted Theo trying to wake her. It was only when he'd started to panic, and become louder and more agitated, that people had taken notice. But by then, Daisy was probably already dead.

"Sergeant, you're back," said Inspector Evans, standing in the doorway of the team room. "I'd like you to interview Theo Watson with me, but I warn you, he's lawyered up."

"Do you think he has something to hide?" Keya asked in a thoughtful tone.

"I've no idea. But that's what we need to find out."

When Keya entered the stark interview room, she thought Theo still looked to be in shock, but the grey walls didn't help. Unlike when she had seen him earlier at the standing stones, he was sitting up so Keya could now see his whole face. He was handsome, in a roguish sort of way, with a heart-shaped face, chubby cheeks and his fair hair was short on the sides but longer on top.

His white collared shirt was crumpled after spending the night outdoors.

Inspector Evans programmed the recording equipment and then said, "Present are myself, Inspector Dai Evans."

"Sergeant Keya Varma."

When Theo didn't speak, his lawyer, a hawkish looking man with round wire-rimmed glasses balanced on his prominent nose, said, "Rupert Sanderson and my client, Theodore Watson."

"Thank you, Mr Sanderson," uttered Inspector Evans. "And for the record, your client is not under arrest. We are trying to establish how Daisy Bentham died and what events led up to her death. We understand your client was with her at the Rollright Standing Stones all last night."

"Yes. I was," Theo answered in a resigned tone. He focused his gaze on Keya, and she realised he had small but intense eyes. "How did she die?" he pleaded.

"We're not sure," Keya replied in a kindly tone. "And we won't know until after the post-mortem."

"Which is being conducted as we speak," Inspector Evans confirmed. "I checked with our crime scene technician before this interview and, so far, there is no obvious cause of death."

"So are you saying she died of natural causes, Inspector?" asked the lawyer.

"No, I'm not. I'm saying that no clear cause of death has been found yet."

Keya looked at Theo and said, "I'm so sorry. I met Daisy last week, and I was thinking of using her bread at my cafe. It's delicious."

"I hope you still will," Theo replied, and he gave her a sad, fleeting smile. "Daisy would want that, although I've no idea who'll run the bakery now she's…" he faltered and gulped in air, before finishing simply with, "gone."

"Was it her idea to open the bakery?" Keya asked.

"It was an idea we both developed. Daisy started baking bread to showcase our flour at events, and it proved so popular we thought we should do more. The bakery was more about marketing the mill than about being profitable itself, but Daisy had done so well and, with the commercial clients she was attracting, I was sure it would soon be in the black."

"And you and Daisy lived together?"

"Yes, in the mill manager's house beside the stream, along the lane from the mill. I like to be close to work, especially at the height of the season when we operate round the clock. Daisy loved the garden, and she'd started redecorating the house. Nothing expensive, but the previous manager had lived there for over fifty years and the interior was rather dated. My uncle extended the kitchen before I moved in, but the rest of it was up to me. To us." Theo sniffed again.

Inspector Evans sat back in his blue chair. He seemed content for Keya to continue.

She went on, "I spoke to some of the people in the village today and they all said Daisy was well liked."

"Of course she was. She was such a wonderful person who always had time for everyone. She liked to walk to the bakery so she could stop to talk to the people she met. And she loved being outside, in the fresh air."

"So you don't know of any reason someone would want to hurt her?"

"No, of course not. Why would they do that? Are you saying someone killed her?" Theo's voice rose in volume.

"No, Mr Watson," Inspector Evans pacified him. "We're not making any assumptions. But your girlfriend's death is suspicious, and we need to establish the facts, while they are fresh in everyone's memory."

The lawyer cleared his throat. "My client is clearly upset. If you've finished questioning him ..."

"Let's move on to yesterday evening," interrupted the Inspector. "What time did you and Daisy arrive at the standing stones?"

Theo looked levelly at the inspector and replied, "We left the house at half past seven and walked through the village and up the hill. I offered to drive but Daisy said it was such a lovely evening, we should walk. And we weren't the only ones. We met Aurora and Viv on the path."

The inspector sat back again so Keya could continue the questioning.

She asked, "So you arrived at the standing stones around eight?"

"I guess so."

"And was it busy?"

"Fairly. People weren't just at the stone circles. They were walking along the edge of the field to the Whispering Knights tomb, which is another group of stones, while others were in the woods or sitting around eating and drinking." Theo stopped and looked directly at her. "I should probably tell you that it wasn't my idea to go to the solstice event. In fact, I would have been much happier staying at home and having an early night. We're currently preparing the mill for harvest season and there's a lot of work to do."

"So it was Daisy's idea?"

"Yes, and she was so excited that I agreed to go with her. I was actually quite relieved when she finished dancing around the fire and told me she felt tired. I suggested we find a spot to sit down, so we did, inside the stone circle. We happily sat together watching the fire as darkness fell and then she closed her eyes and rested her head on my shoulder. I covered us both with blankets and I must have dozed off as well."

Theo's gaze dropped, and Keya thought he was considering the night's events.

"I kept waking during the night and when I did, there were always people talking softly and some were even wandering about near the fire. The atmosphere was pleasant and peaceful, but also with an undertone of anticipation. Although the sun didn't rise until nearly five, it was getting light from around four and people were moving about and preparing for it. That's when I tried to wake Daisy. But I couldn't."

Theo gulped before continuing in a dry voice, "I removed our blankets and shook her, but her eyes remained closed. I think I started to panic. I know an elderly lady with a bright yellow headscarf came to help. She told me Daisy was dead. But I didn't believe her. She tried to drag me away, but I stayed with Daisy, waiting for her to wake up."

Keya waited for Theo to continue.

"Then Dr Reid arrived and spoke to the woman. He also told me Daisy was dead. I think I let the woman take me away, but only because Dr Reid promised to look after Daisy. I'm not really sure what happened after that. Are you sure Daisy really is dead?"

Theo looked at Keya, his small eyes intense and pleading.

Keya drew her lips together and nodded. As she watched Theo, she couldn't believe he'd harmed Daisy, unless he was an exceptional actor.

Inspector Evans declared, "Interview terminated at 13.07."

CHAPTER FIFTEEN

Keya thought Gilly and Aunt Beanie both looked their age when she walked into the interview room and saw them sitting on the other side of the grey Formica table. But it might have been the harsh office light reflected off the table and the grey walls.

"Thanks for coming in, but it's best we do this properly," Keya said as she placed her notepad and pen on the table and pulled out a chair.

As she sat down, she asked, "Do you mind if we record the interview?"

Neither woman replied, so Keya keyed the relevant information into the recording equipment, including the date and the location.

Aunt Beanie asked, "Have you discovered how the poor girl died?"

"The result of the post-mortem is inconclusive. Officially, she died because her heart stopped, but isn't that what happens when someone dies?"

"I suppose so," Gilly muttered.

Using her professional voice, Keya stated, "Interview commenced. Present are Sergeant Keya Varma."

She looked at Gilly and Aunt Beanie and instructed, "Please say your names for the recording."

"Bernadette Devereux," said Aunt Beanie, loudly.

Gilly mumbled, "Gilly Wimsey."

Keya continued, "Returning to the cause of death of Daisy Bentham, the pathologist couldn't find a reason for her heart to stop. There's no degeneration of her heart muscles to suggest she had a weak heart and was susceptible to a heart attack. There was a considerable amount of fluid in her lungs, but the pathologist couldn't say if that caused the heart attack, or was a result of it. Blood has been sent for analysis, but Sujin says it could take at least a week to receive the results as the lab has a backlog of cases. He's also requested a blood sample so he can perform some of the tests himself."

"I can't understand how it happened," stated Aunt Beanie. "I didn't see anyone near the girl apart from Theo, and he's clearly devastated by what happened. It must be some sort of freak accident."

The door opened, and Stan carried in two mugs of tea for Gilly and Aunt Beanie.

"Keya?" he asked.

"I'm fine, thanks. I've just had one."

After Inspector Evans had terminated their previous interview with Theo Watson, the solicitor had insisted on leaving with his client and, as there was no crime to charge him with, the inspector complied.

And Keya agreed with Aunt Beanie. Theo did appear to have idolised Daisy and was devastated by her death.

Aunt Beanie sipped her tea, but Gilly sat despondently and left hers untouched on the table.

Keya decided it was best to get the interview over and done with. "What time did you arrive at the standing stones yesterday evening?" she asked.

"Just after eight," Aunt Beanie replied. "Gilly invited me over to hers for an early supper with Peter and the kids. Then we left them to clear up, and I drove us both to the stones."

"And did you notice anything unusual?"

"What's normal about grown people wearing garlands of flowers and dancing barefoot, playing pipes, or singing ancient songs? But the atmosphere was very peaceful and harmonious, if that's what you're getting at."

"When did you first notice Daisy?"

"About half an hour later. Gilly and I set our chairs up beside the largest stone and enjoyed a cup of tea. Gilly had baked some scones, and I had a pot of Norman's homemade raspberry jam. We enjoyed them together while we people-watched. Groups of them sat or stood in and around the stones, and others were in the woods at the edge of the field. Couples, mostly, if you get my drift?"

"Er no, I don't."

Gilly looked up and said in a flat tone, "The solstice is about nature, love, and abundance."

Finally, the penny dropped. "Oh, I see what you mean. Did Daisy and Theo emerge from the wood together?" Keya enquired.

"Yes, and Daisy was straightening her skirt," Gilly added unemotionally.

Keya made a note on her pad to check if the pathologist's report mentioned any signs of recent sexual activity.

"But she was a lovely figure, dancing beside the fire as the pipes played," Gilly said in a dreamy voice.

"Did you see her eat, drink, or smoke anything?" Keya asked.

Aunt Beanie and Gilly looked at each other.

"She was holding a can at one point, wasn't she?" Gilly queried.

"I believe so, and I think I saw her smoking, but I had the impression it wasn't a regular cigarette," replied Aunt Beanie, addressing Gilly.

"Do you think that killed her? That she was poisoned?" Gilly spoke to Aunt Beanie, but they both turned and stared at Keya for an answer.

"That is something we need to look into. Thank you." Then Keya asked, "What else did you see relating to Daisy, or those she was with?"

"She chatted to plenty of people, but as the light started to fade, I heard her say she was feeling tired, and Theo helped her to a stone where they both sat down. I have to say, after that, I didn't really take much notice of either her or Theo. We watched the campfire, and I did my turn adding wood from the pile beside it," Aunt Beanie said.

She then added, "And that lady who runs the shop in Lower Rollright stood up and gave a brief history of the stones and then said we could buy merchandise at her shop."

"Her friend with the black hair read a few people's palms by torchlight, and there were those young women who read poetry. It was lovely, but I think it sent me to sleep," Gilly confessed.

"I dozed off eventually, but slept fitfully," Aunt Beanie admitted. "But whenever I woke, everything was quiet and peaceful. There were always people awake, but they whispered to each other so as not to disturb those who were sleeping."

Keya concluded, "So you didn't see or witness anything unusual or untoward in the evening or during the night? What about this morning?"

"The camp started to come alive around four. Gilly and I had a cup of tea and a sandwich, and I went for a stroll, as I was stiff from sleeping in the camping chair. A few women were performing yoga, so I made a half-hearted attempt to join in. I wasn't any good, but at least I had a stretch," Aunt Beanie said.

"I walked down to the farm shop to use the facilities," said Gilly. "And I returned around twenty to five and found Aunt Beanie trying to calm Theo down."

Aunt Beanie took up the narrative. "As I was returning from my half-hearted attempt at yoga, I passed in front of the stone where Daisy was sitting. Theo was leaning over and shaking her and kept saying, 'wake up'. Of course she didn't. Even in the dim light, I could tell by her pallor that she was dead. But Theo couldn't, and he was starting to panic. I stepped in and checked for a pulse, praying there was one, but of course there wasn't. I tried to drag Theo away, but he insisted on staying with Daisy. That's when I asked Gilly to call you."

Some of the colour had returned to Gilly's cheeks, and she said in a business-like tone, "There was no phone signal at the stones, so I went back to the farm shop and called you from there. I bought two coffees, which I carried back to Beanie, and then we waited for you."

"And Theo?" Keya asked.

"I think he was in shock," Aunt Beanie replied. "He wouldn't leave Daisy's body until a man in a trilby hat arrived and said he'd stay with her. We did manage to get half a cup of tea into him, but nothing more. He just sat in the camping chair moaning, his head in his hands."

"And the other people?" Keya asked.

Gilly, whose cheeks now had a rosy tint to them, replied, "There were new arrivals for sunrise, but it didn't take long for people to realise there was a dead body. Oh, and I'd forgotten about the boy."

"What boy?" asked Keya.

"A youth with a shaved head. He went to talk to Daisy but when he realised she was dead, he started shouting into the crowd. That was when the atmosphere changed. I'm not sure what happened next," admitted Gilly, "as I left to call you."

Keya remembered Ash, the shaven-headed lad who'd come into the bakery.

"Was he wearing black?" Keya asked.

"Actually he was, which was strange amongst all the brightly coloured outfits, but at least he had a light coloured T-shirt under the black jacket," Gilly remembered. "Pale green I think."

"What happened when people realised there was a dead body?" Keya thought she already knew the answer.

"They left," Aunt Beanie said. "Said the solstice was cursed. Most of the people who'd waited all night stayed, but not all of them. Some packed up, but others, like the woman with the shop in the village, were visibly excited."

"But people thought it was a hoax," Gilly said. "I heard them discussing what they thought was a publicity stunt for the standing stones. For that woman's shop." Gilly shook her head and said in a small voice, "But it wasn't a hoax, was it?"

CHAPTER SIXTEEN

At the end of the interview, Keya asked Gilly, "Can I take your phone and download the photos you took this morning?"

Gilly retrieved her phone from a large leather handbag and pressed some keys before sliding it across the table to Keya.

Keya swiped through the photos until she came across one of Gilly's children, Thomas and Olivia. Stopping, she clicked on all the photos after the children and sent them to herself. She'd pass them on to Sujin.

"Thanks," she said, handing the phone back.

The interview complete, Keya escorted Aunt Beanie and Gilly out of the police station.

"You will keep us updated, won't you?" pleaded Gilly, as she stood on the concrete entrance steps.

Rays of sunshine warmed Keya's face.

"I'll tell you what I can," Keya agreed.

"And how was the play last night?" Aunt Beanie asked. "I haven't seen Dotty to ask her if you had a chance to look round the gardens?"

"During the interval we followed a trail through the woods and gardens, and saw acrobats, a fire-eater, and a mermaid."

Aunt Beanie's eyes widened and then she realised, "Of course, in the stone plunge pool."

"I did enjoy the play, although I found it a bit silly, which wasn't what I was expecting from Shakespeare," Keya admitted.

"That's a shame," Aunt Beanie sympathised.

"But it was still a fun night, and we had a lovely picnic. And now I better get back to work."

"Of course. We shouldn't keep you chatting when you're investigating the death of a young woman. But pop in sometime when you visit Dotty."

Aunt Beanie and Gilly walked away as Keya turned and re-entered the police station. She found the team room full and as she pushed past Stan to reach her desk, Inspector Evans said, "And now Sergeant Varma has joined us, we can begin."

"Sorry, sir," Keya muttered as she sat down behind her desk. Sujin was seated at his old desk, next to Ryan, and Stan was leaning against it.

Sitting at the desk next to Keya was one of the young officers she recognised from the crime scene.

Inspector Evans, who continued to wear his brown suit jacket in spite of the hot, sticky atmosphere of the team room, was standing in the doorway to his office.

Keya rolled up the sleeves of her white shirt and remembered she needed to wash her short-sleeved ones.

"First, I'd like to introduce Constable Warren Sparrow, who's been seconded to our team for the duration of this investigation."

Constable Sparrow looked barely older than Gilly's son, Thomas. He was thin, with a narrow face and a mop of dark curls. And he looked absolutely petrified.

Everyone murmured their version of "Hello," and "Welcome".

"Back to the case," instructed Inspector Evans. "Sergeant Varma, what have you discovered during your interviews?"

"The accounts all add up, sir. The victim was happy yesterday evening and enjoying herself up at the standing stones until, just before dark, she complained of being tired, and her boyfriend, Theo Watson, helped her to sit down by a stone. The following morning, he tried to wake her, but he couldn't because she was dead."

Inspector Evans raised his eyebrows and said, "Very succinctly put." He turned to Sujin and asked, "What can you tell us about the post-mortem?"

"Daisy Bentham died between midnight and two am, when her heart stopped beating. The reason for this has not yet been established, but there was no sign of trauma or bleeding, internal or external. The only anomaly is a large amount of fluid in her lungs, but that could have happened after her heart stopped, particularly as she was in a sitting position. Blood has been sent to the lab and I've also asked for a sample to test. Perhaps the answer will lie there."

"Witnesses saw her drinking from a can and smoking something they didn't think was a cigarette," Keya added.

"I have an empty cider can and the butt of a roll-up, which I'll test," Sujin responded.

The inspector cleared his throat before asking, "Could this just be a simple heart attack? It does happen to young, seemingly healthy people."

"A sudden cardiac arrest can occur, but the post-mortem would have highlighted the reason for it," Sujin responded. "Either blocked arteries or the heart muscle being too thick or too hard. There was nothing like that in this case, so something else caused her heart to stop."

Inspector Evans scratched the bald part of his head. "But we have no idea what? Or how? Or if anyone else was involved? Sergeant, have you discovered anyone who'd want to harm our victim?"

"She was well liked," Keya replied. "She did fall out with her father over her boyfriend, Theo Watson, and he kicked her out of his house. But she moved into the mill manager's house with Theo, and they seemed happy. And she'd recently opened a bakery in the village."

Ryan added, "The dad's a slob, and we know he likes to spend time in the pub. I don't think he would have been easy to live with after Daisy's mother left him for another man."

"She's back in the village, too. Doreen Skinner, she's called, but I got the impression she's no longer with Mr Skinner," said Keya. "She heard about the death in the village early this morning and walked up to the standing stones. She was very upset."

"Inspector Sue is with her now," Inspector Evans revealed. "And then Sue's going to see the father and younger sister."

"She's a funny one, sir. The sister," Ryan said.

"Because she believes in fairies?" Keya asked him. "She does spend a lot of time with Aurora and Viv, and she probably needs somewhere to escape to rather than spending all her time looking after her father, but I know what you mean."

"She said she'd killed her sister, because she prayed to the fairies to bring her home, and Daisy had refused them," Ryan explained.

Inspector Evans rolled his eyes.

"We know fairies didn't kill Daisy," Keya said, frustration seeping into her voice.

"But something supernatural appears to have done. What other explanation is there?" Ryan asked, his voice sincere.

The room was silent.

Then Keya asked, "Sujin, was there evidence of any sexual activity before her death?" She tried to remain professional, but she felt her cheeks burn.

"Yes. Do you think that's important? That she was assaulted? There is no sign of bruising or …"

"No, I think it was consensual. I just wanted to check. Theo didn't mention it, but he was still in a state of shock."

"Where do we go from here, sir?" Ryan asked.

"I'd like you to look into her bank records, her phone calls, her computer if she had one, and any social media accounts. Sergeant Varma and Constable Sparrow should check the crime scene again, now that everyone has left, not that I think you'll find anything." He looked at Keya.

"And then we'll continue interviewing anyone who's been in contact with the victim recently, starting with her mother."

Inspector Evans looked round the room and sighed. "This may lead nowhere, but in case there is something that the post-mortem has missed, we need to ensure we have followed the correct procedure and, more importantly, that we do everything to bring justice to Daisy Bentham."

CHAPTER SEVENTEEN

Keya drove Constable Wayne Sparrow to the Rollright Standing Stones. "What do you know about this case?" she asked.

"A young woman died during the night, and we need to establish how, and if, someone killed her."

"Yes, I suppose that is correct, although at this stage we need to question if anyone else was involved or not. We shouldn't just jump to the conclusion that she was murdered. At least not until we have the full results of the post-mortem."

Several cars were parked in the first lay-by beside the field where the standing stones were located, but Keya managed to find a space in the second one between a silver Mini and a white Toyota Yaris.

Entering the coppice, Keya noticed a full black dustbin bag propped up against a fence post and, when she entered the grassy area beyond it, she spotted a small thin figure collecting rubbish inside the circle of stones.

Striding forward, she called, "Dora," and the figure stopped and looked up. Keya ducked under the flapping white and blue police tape and approached Dora Potts, who was standing beside another open, black dustbin bag.

"What are you doing?" Keya asked.

"Someone has to tidy up," Dora replied in a defiant voice, showing a steely side to her character. "They call themselves new age and at one with nature, but they're still happy to leave all their litter behind. Look at this."

Dora picked up a plastic energy drink bottle. "How long do you think it will take to decompose? And left out here, it'll blow about and get stuck in a tree or a hedgerow, or some poor animal might try to eat it."

"But this is a crime scene," Keya said, with a note of understanding. She was also frustrated by younger generations calling for changes to environmental policy while happily using their mobile phones, leaving the lights on, and dropping their rubbish. And someone like Dora, from the generation they complained about, was left to tidy up after them.

Dora glared at Constable Sparrow when he joined them, as if he was personally responsible for all the debris.

"What crime?" Dora protested.

"Daisy's death."

"That was unfortunate, but it isn't a crime to die."

"It is if someone else is involved," Keya responded.

Dora's eyes widened, and her mouth formed a silent O.

"I'm not saying anyone was," Keya continued. "We still aren't certain of the cause of death but, until we are, we have to treat this as a suspicious death. My colleague, Constable Sparrow, will take that dustbin bag from you, as he'll need to sort through it, and I'm afraid I'll have to ask you to leave the standing stones."

"When can I finish tidying up? We can't leave it like this. What will visitors say?" Dora demanded.

"Hopefully there won't be too many visitors over the next few days and the police tape will keep those who do come away from this area." Keya turned to Constable Sparrow and said, "When you take the rubbish bags to the car, can you collect the three plastic fence posts I put in the boot, and the roll of tape, so we can make the cordon more secure?"

Constable Sparrow took the black bag from Dora, who glowered at Keya.

Keya regarded Dora thoughtfully. She wasn't just the diminutive figure she liked people to think she was. "What did you think of Daisy

Bentham?"

"She was a jumped-up little madam."

Keya stepped back, surprised by the bitterness in Dora's voice. But she waited for Dora to expand.

"Moving into Mill House and announcing her grand plans to the whole village. Redecorating and updating, she called it," spat Dora. "And that wonderful garden."

"Do you know it?" asked Keya.

"Know it? I designed it. I lived there for fifty years."

"But I thought the old mill manager lived there?" Keya queried in an uncertain tone.

"He did. He was my father, Sir Anthony's younger brother, and we lived at Mill House as a family. My mother died young, and I looked after Daddy until he became too ill to work. And then Sir Anthony threw us out and installed Dorothy's son as the new manager."

"Dorothy?" Keya was confused.

"Yes, Dorothy Watson. She's Sir Anthony and my father's younger sister."

"So you are Sir Anthony's niece?"

"Yes, but so what?" Dora asked defensively.

"Nothing. I'm just trying to understand where everyone fits in. And your father?"

"Dead. Less than a year after we moved out of Mill House."

"But you still live in the village?"

"Yes, number five, Barley Row. And that's another thing. Daisy should never have upped and left like that, leaving her poor, dreamy sister to cope with their father. Dennis Bentham is a brute. I can't blame Doreen for leaving him."

Constable Sparrow appeared carrying three blue plastic posts and a roll of tape. As he reached the crime scene cordon, he bent down to duck under it and dropped everything.

"Stay there, Constable," Keya called. "I'll help you in a minute." She turned back to Dora, but the slight figure had already left the stone circle and was hurrying towards the edge of the coppice. She deftly ducked under the crime scene tape and disappeared amongst the trees.

But at least Keya knew where she lived.

Keya and Constable Sparrow spent the next hour at the standing stones. They reinforced the police cordon with the extra plastic poles and lengths of blue and white tape. They then searched the scene. First inside the stone circle, although Dora had efficiently tidied most of the rubbish away, and then outside it.

"Eugh," Constable Sparrow exclaimed as he found something unsavoury in the perimeter wood.

Keya was examining the ribbons, bells and pieces of writing attached to the branches of an oak tree which stood on the edge of the wood nearest the standing stones.

Hanging from a green ribbon, there was a card with the image of an oak tree at sunrise and below it the words for a summer solstice blessing. It looked like something Aurora might sell in her shop.

Keya no longer felt a chill when she re-entered the stone circle. Perhaps she'd imagined it before. After all she'd been only too quick to point out to Ryan that there were no such thing as ancient mystical forces. But then?

A lone blackbird sang in the low branches of a tree, and she felt at peace.

Looking around, she said to Constable Sparrow, "There's nothing more for us here."

She didn't know why, but she was certain that the answer to Daisy's death did not lie at the Standing Stones.

Something stopped her before she stepped out of the stone circle and she knew, with absolute certainty, that Daisy had not died from natural causes.

CHAPTER EIGHTEEN

Keya felt a little disconcerted after she left the standing stones and drove Constable Sparrow down to Lower Rollright.

She had no evidence, no proof that Daisy's death was due to anything other than natural causes. But it was as if a voice had whispered to her, shouted even, while she stood inside the standing stones, and it was too insistent for her to ignore.

But she could hardly return to the station and announce that spirits at the standing stones had told her Daisy's death was suspicious. As always, she needed to undertake this investigation as she would any other and, by doing so, discover the truth.

"Where did you say Daisy's mother, Mrs Skinner, lived?" Keya asked Constable Sparrow.

"In a property provided by the mill, where she works," answered the young, curly-haired constable.

"That'll be Stone Circle Flour. I haven't been there yet, but I think it's on the other side of the stream, across the bridge."

Keya passed Mrs Reid's Rollright Stores and slowed as she approached the narrow stone bridge. She wasn't certain there was room for two vehicles, so she waited patiently as a white van took the bridge too fast and swerved to avoid her.

"Idiot," she muttered as she drove over the bridge.

"Aren't you going to stop him for driving dangerously?" asked Constable Sparrow.

"I doubt he was exceeding the speed limit, and I'm not sure that chasing him across the Cotswolds to give him a warning is the best use of my time. I doubt he'd take much notice, anyway."

They approached the entrance to the mill with a large cream sign informing them they had arrived at Stone Circle Flour.

The original three-storey, Cotswold stone mill building had been incorporated into a larger complex. The first building they passed was a large open-fronted shed with wooden pallets stacked up at one end. Between it and the old stone building was a cylindrical metal tower and a tall metal building with rows of slats instead of windows.

After the mill complex, the paved road turned into a narrow track and Keya drove for another hundred metres until they arrived at two tall stone buildings, each with four cream-painted front doors.

"I think these must be the mill workers' accommodation," Keya said, peering through the windscreen.

"There's another property further along," Constable Sparrow pointed out.

"That might be the manager's house." Keya wondered if she should request a warrant to search through Daisy's possessions. Now Theo had a lawyer, he might not let her inside, but she might still try. "Do we know which one is Mrs Skinner's?"

"Her address is 1 Mill Cottage."

Keya, accompanied by a nervous Constable Sparrow, rang the doorbell beside the first cream door. A floral curtain in the downstairs window twitched and less than a minute later the door opened, and a gaunt, blotchy red face peered out at them.

"If you're looking for your colleague, she left half an hour ago," Doreen Skinner said.

"Actually, we'd like to speak to you, and ask you some questions," Keya said, trying to sound both professional and empathetic.

"Sue said you would. Come in," Doreen invited, submissively.

Doreen led them into a narrow corridor and through into a small high-ceilinged living room with a stained, green, two-seater sofa and a matching armchair. A lingering smell of vinegar hung in the air.

Doreen sat in the armchair and Keya sat at right angles to her on one half of the sofa.

Constable Sparrow hovered.

"Sit down, Constable," Keya instructed before she opened her notepad. Since Inspector Sue had already visited Doreen in her role as the family liaison officer, Keya decided to skip the part about being sorry for Doreen's loss.

"We're sorry to intrude, but we do need more details about your daughter and your relationship with her for our investigation."

Keya noticed Doreen wince when she mentioned relationship, but she'd come back to that. First, she wanted her interviewee to feel comfortable so she could build a rapport with her.

"This is a lovely village to grow up in. From everything I've heard, I presume Daisy was a happy child."

Doreen smiled and relaxed into the armchair. "Oh, she was."

For the next ten minutes, Keya let Doreen tell her stories of Daisy's happy childhood in the area and at school in nearby Chipping Norton.

"I thought Daisy would be a nurse, or work with animals. She was always so kind and thoughtful, but after school she got stuck here. It was Dennis' fault. He wouldn't let her go. When I came back four years ago, Daisy was working in the pub and helping Dennis with his accounts and running his business. He's a plumber, you see."

Doreen looked down at her hands. "I tried to persuade her to leave. If not to study, at least to work somewhere else, even if it was just Oxford or Cheltenham. But she said she wouldn't leave Dennis and Zoe."

Doreen slowly shook her head. "I should have offered to have Zoe live with me, but I doubt she would have done. She blamed me for leaving them. She didn't understand what I went through married to Dennis."

"When did you leave?" Keya asked.

"Eight years ago. I met a salesman at one of the holiday cottages I cleaned. I thought I was escaping my life here but, in reality, it was just another abusive relationship and when he hit me, well, that was the final straw. I walked out. But I had nowhere to go."

Doreen smiled sadly at Keya. "I thought Dennis would have me back, but he's a stubborn one. After a couple of weeks at the pub, I was running out of money. That's when Sir Anthony offered me a job at the mill, and as it came with this pokey cottage, I agreed."

Keya glanced around. She actually thought there was more room here than in the cottage where Dennis and Zoe lived.

"And you returned?" Keya enquired, her pen poised over her notebook.

"As I said, four years ago. I thought I'd sort things out with Dennis, but here I am, still packing flour at the mill and seeing less and less of my girls. And Daisy ..."

Doreen caught herself before continuing in a stiff voice, "She did well for herself and moved into Mill House when Dennis chucked her out. And last year she opened the bakery. She was going places."

Keya couldn't decide if Doreen was happy or resentful of Daisy's success. She remembered how Doreen had flinched when she'd said the word 'relationship'.

Doreen continued, "Meanwhile, Zoe is in the clutches of the two witches, and I can't seem to do anything about it."

"Witches?" Constable Sparrow queried.

"I presume you mean Aurora and Viv?" Keya added quickly.

"I do." Doreen folded her arms.

"And you and Daisy? How well did you get on?"

"Fine." Doreen sat back and crossed her arms.

"Had the two of you had an argument, or fallen out about anything?"

"Who told you that? They're lying."

"Nobody," Keya reassured her. She thought she'd better move the interview on to the unpleasant topic of Daisy's death. "Mrs Skinner, Doreen, do you know anyone who'd want to hurt Daisy?"

"Hurt her?" cried Doreen. "Of course not."

"But someone might have been jealous of her living in the big house, with Sir Anthony's nephew, and opening the bakery. She was doing well for herself, as you pointed out. And the garden ..."

"You've been speaking to Dora, haven't you?" Doreen narrowed her eyes.

"We met her up at the standing stones."

"She was jealous of Daisy. But then, like me, she lives in a pokey cottage while Daisy lives, lived," choked Doreen, "at the big house.

And she had plans for it. She was going to completely redecorate it. She'd already redesigned most of the garden. Oh, and it is a lovely garden going down to the stream. All I have here are a few flagstones and the trees shade the evening sun."

"And Dora was jealous?"

"Furious, although you wouldn't know it. She's very good at hiding her feelings and pretending to be everyone's helpful friend. But I don't blame her. She misses her family. She and her dad were together a long time. And I can understand how she feels."

CHAPTER NINETEEN

When Doreen returned to stories of Daisy's idyllic childhood, Keya decided it was time to leave.

"Thank you, Doreen, but we need to continue our investigation," Keya said, standing up.

Doreen remained seated, and she looked paler as she asked, "Do you really think someone hurt Daisy?"

"We don't know, and until we do, we have to continue the investigation in a professional manner." Keya hoped she sounded reassuring rather than bureaucratic.

She wasn't sure she did as Doreen's eyes began to water, and her chin quivered.

"There's no need to get up," Keya said quickly. "We can show ourselves out."

Outside, in the fresh air, Constable Sparrow said, "It must be awful as a mum to lose your daughter."

Keya nodded. "I think some people believe it's easier when they are grown up, and no longer a child, but I suspect the sense of loss is just as strong."

Keya's phone pinged, and she checked her messages.

"It's Ryan," she said. "He wants us to find any electronic equipment Daisy had, like a tablet or laptop. Which means we do need to visit her home. Let's see if it's the building you spotted earlier."

Returning to Keya's police car, they drove a hundred metres up the road until they arrived at a large two-storey stone house. A climbing yellow rose bush was in bloom on the wall beside the front door, which was painted a slightly lighter shade of yellow.

Keya pushed open a wooden garden gate and walked up the short flagstone path to the front door. Beside it, a cream oval plaque said simply 'Mill House'.

"This is the right one, then," Constable Sparrow confirmed beside her.

Failing to find a doorbell, Keya rapped on the door with a black knocker in the shape of a sheaf of wheat.

It was some time before the crumpled figure of Theo Watson opened the door.

"I'm sorry to disturb you," Keya said, and this time her voice was sincere. "But we need to look through Daisy's things. In particular, we need any electronic items."

Without saying a word, Theo turned and walked back inside the house.

Keya and Constable Sparrow followed him, and the young constable stopped and closed the front door.

An antique looking red carpet ran across the flagstone floor in the hall.

"Her laptop and tablet should be in there," Theo said, inclining his head towards an open doorway.

"And her phone is upstairs on the bedside table. Are you OK sorting yourselves out?"

"Of course," Keya replied, hiding her satisfaction at being able to look around the property by herself.

The living room was well proportioned with dark wood and antique furniture. Two dated but attractive cream sofas with flowers on them faced each other in the centre of the room. A wooden blanket box was between them with magazines scattered on top of it. There was also a silver-coloured laptop, and next to it a tablet in a light blue case.

"Can you bag those?" Keya instructed Constable Sparrow, as she slowly walked around the perimeter of the room. A vase of summer flowers stood on a table next to a casement window, out of which Keya was able to see the garden, which both Dora and Daisy had been so passionate about. It looked colourful with bushes and flowerbeds. To the right, there was a sheltered section with a small pond and a garden bench. It did look a peaceful place to sit.

On another table there was a collection of silver-framed photographs of Theo through the various stages of his life, and at the front, one of him and a smiling Daisy dressed up for a wedding or party. She took a photo of it with her phone.

Overall, the room was pleasant and welcoming, although as she walked out, she noticed a brown stain on the ceiling and a section of peeling, faded wallpaper.

Upstairs consisted of several unoccupied rooms. A couple of them were being used to store boxes and a collection of furniture, golf clubs, and other bits and pieces. There was a neat double bedroom, which she thought was a spare room, and at the back, with views over the garden, was the larger master bedroom.

From there, Keya could see the garden path meandering down to the stream and what looked like a metal egg-shaped swing suspended from an old oak tree. She could imagine a carefree Daisy relaxing in it.

The bedroom contained a large sleigh-style bed which was neatly made with a well-loved pony soft toy on one pillow. On the retro-looking wooden bedside table lay a phone in a cream case with Stone Circle Flour and Bakery printed on it.

Keya picked it up with a gloved hand and turned it over. The screen was blank, so it probably needed charging.

She also noticed the lamp, and she recognised the romance book next to it. How long was it since she'd had the time to read?

The wardrobe contained a collection of smarter menswear and dresses, and the chest of drawers, the expected underwear, tops, jeans, and trousers. All was as it should be, apart from the fact that one of the room's occupants would never return.

The normality of the room, and its readiness to welcome Daisy back, hit Keya more than anything else had done and she felt her chest constrict.

Was it because someone so young had lost her life? Or that Daisy really didn't deserve to die?

"Anything else, Sergeant?" Constable Sparrow asked from the doorway.

"Just this phone," she choked. "And then wait for me downstairs in the hall. There's one more thing I need to ask Mr Watson."

For some reason, having spent time in Daisy's bedroom, Keya felt comfortable enough to ask Theo, "Did you and Daisy have sex up at the standing stones?"

They were standing in a light, airy kitchen with new pale-yellow kitchen units and modern kitchen appliances.

Theo leaned against the wooden counter, his eyes widening and then misting over. "Daisy wanted a baby, and she thought the standing stones on the eve of the summer solstice was the perfect place to conceive. And we weren't the only ones," sniffed Theo. "Several other couples were also in the woods."

He looked at Keya with a forlorn expression. "And now Daisy will never have her baby."

CHAPTER TWENTY

It was late afternoon by the time Keya and Constable Sparrow returned to Cirencester Police Station. Keya yawned as she walked along the corridor towards the team room.

"Keeping you up, Keya?" Stan joked as he stepped out of the small kitchenette.

"It's been a long day," Keya replied, as she led Constable Sparrow into the team room.

Finding Ryan at his desk, she said, "I can't believe it was only last night that we watched the play."

"I know. Did you find any electronics for me?" He eyed the transparent evidence bags Constable Sparrow was carrying enthusiastically. Why wasn't he affected by his lack of sleep?

Turning to Constable Sparrow, Keya said, "Give the laptop and tablet to Ryan, but I'll take the phone down to Sujin. And then you should go home. You've also had a long day."

"Thanks, Sergeant." Constable Sparrow grinned at her before stepping in front of Ryan's desk.

She left the two of them chatting and headed towards the custody suite, where Sujin had a small workroom.

He usually listened to music to counter the noise of protesting or drunk people who'd been arrested and were being processed in the adjacent custody suite, and this afternoon it sounded like a classical track playing on the other side of the closed door.

She knocked and entered.

Sujin looked up, smiled, and asked, "To what do I owe this visit?"

"Does there have to be a reason?" Keya protested.

Sujin's smile broadened. "Not at all. Have you just popped in to see me?"

Keya looked down at the evidence bag she was carrying and, feeling contrite, replied, "Actually, I've brought you Daisy's phone. I think it needs charging."

When she looked up, she noticed a fleeting look of disappointment in Sujin's eyes before he smiled slowly and said, "Thank you. I'll charge it and see what I can find on it. Anything in particular you're looking for?"

"Any death threats would be helpful," Keya considered grimly, "but aside from those, any unusual activity. You know the sort of thing."

Keya turned and felt Sujin's hand on her arm.

"Have I upset you?" he asked, his voice full of concern.

Keya turned back and her shoulders slumped. "She was so young, and full of life and hope." Keya felt the tears welling up. "And she wanted a baby. That's why she and Theo were in the woods. She wanted to conceive on the eve of the summer solstice."

She blinked, and as she did, she felt a pair of strong arms encircle her. Resting her head on Sujin's chest, she sobbed. For Daisy, or for herself? She wasn't sure.

Eventually, she sniffed and pulled back. Wiping her eyes with the sleeve of her white shirt, she apologised, "Sorry. I didn't mean to get all emotional on you."

"I'm pleased that you did." Sujin stopped and then continued, "I mean, I'm glad you feel able to open up to me. There are so many stresses and triggers with this job, and often too few outlets to deal with them. Look, I know we both have a lot of work, but it's not going anywhere. Do you fancy grabbing an early bite to eat? I think we're both shattered, and I'll be better tackling all this in the morning after a good night's sleep."

Pulling on a fresh pair of gloves, he opened the evidence bag containing Daisy's phone and manoeuvred it round so the charging point was facing the open end. He connected it to a lead.

Keya used the time to pull herself together. Her little house was welcoming, but it was also empty. And it was too lovely an evening to be stuck inside.

"How about The Swan Hotel at Bibury?" Sujin suggested. "We can choose something from the bar menu and sit out beside the River Coln before it gets too busy."

Keya felt guilty at the mention of the River Coln. She hadn't checked in once with Millie at her cafe, but … "That would be lovely. When do you want to leave?"

"Half an hour?" Sujin suggested.

Back in the team room, Keya found Constable Sparrow and Ryan examining Daisy's laptop and tablet.

"Sergeant," she heard Inspector Evans call through his open office door.

Keya sighed and walked across the room and entered the inspector's office.

He leaned back in his chair and rested his hands behind his head. The sweat stains on his cream shirt were evident, but at least he'd removed his brown suit jacket.

"What progress have you made this afternoon?" he asked.

Keya told him about the visit she and Constable Sparrow had made to the crime scene, their encounter with Dora, and the interview with Daisy's mother.

"We also went to Mill House and collected Daisy's laptop, tablet, and phone. Constable Jenkins is working on them now, with Constable Sparrow, even though I told him to go home. I took Daisy's phone down to Sujin, as it needs charging, and I thought he'd be able to get more from it."

"Good call. And now I think you should take your own advice and go home. Start tomorrow with a clear head and a fresh pair of eyes."

"Yes, sir."

As Keya left the team room with a lighter step, she called, "Goodnight," to Ryan and Constable Sparrow.

Forty-five minutes later, Keya placed a glass of iced mint tea on a wooden table under a timber-framed gazebo beside the River Coln. Colourful baskets of red and yellow flowers were hanging from the timbers which supported the gazebo's slate roof.

She had crossed a wooden footbridge from The Swan Hotel's main gardens to reach this little island of tranquillity. But she wasn't the only one. Several women were laughing as they enjoyed cocktails at a table on the other side of a low stone wall, beside a large pampas grass.

Sitting down, Keya closed her eyes and tried to ignore them, concentrating instead on the sound of the stream. It was like fresh, clear music.

She wished she'd had a floaty summer dress to change into rather than her tight-fitting cotton trousers.

"Sorry, I'm late," Sujin said.

Keya opened her eyes and watched as he manoeuvred a wooden chair around until it was next to hers, facing the river.

"This is a favourite spot of mine," Sujin confessed. "And it helps that the food is great. They also have an outdoor hot tub, which I'm occasionally allowed to use when the hotel is quiet. As I told you, we all need to unwind, and this is one place I've found to do that."

Keya watched as a duck glided past on the water, followed by five ducklings. She picked up her glass and sipped the iced tea. Delicious, with a hint of lime, and the tartness of apple to cut through the sweetness of honey. And overall, the refreshing taste and scent of mint.

"When did you last have a holiday?" Sujin asked.

Keya blinked. A holiday. "I've no idea," she replied. With her police work, and opening and running the cafe, it wasn't something she'd even considered.

"I believe everyone needs to take a break," Sujin said. "It enables the mind to relax and start making connections it doesn't usually have a chance to do. That's also why I like walking. I do some of my best work when I'm wandering through a wood or across a field full of sheep."

Keya considered his comment. He was right, of course. It was just that … "It's not only the time. I don't really want to go away by myself. I'm not sure what I would do."

"What about your friends? Maybe Dotty?" Sujin suggested.

"She's been away for the last year. And now she's studying and setting up her antique business. I'm not sure she'll have the time."

"You don't have to go abroad. There are some wonderful places in the UK to visit. How about Wales, or Scotland, or the Lake District?"

Keya had been to Cardiff, and The Forest of Dean was almost in Wales.

"Don't worry about it now. It's only a suggestion," Sujin said. "And I brought some menus with me." He handed one to Keya.

Most of the dishes were meat-based, although there was a vegetarian pithivier, which was a posh name for a pie. But that was too heavy for a summer night.

"Found anything you fancy?" asked Sujin.

"Um." She looked down at the starters. Mushrooms on toast. Hardly adventurous. Ah, yes, that would do. "Yes, the creamy mushroom tagliatelle with pine nuts, fresh rocket, and parmesan."

Sujin left to order their food inside the hotel, and Keya sat back and sipped her iced tea. She did like the idea of a holiday and wondered if Dotty might have any time off from her course in the summer?

And Sujin was right. They didn't need to go abroad. A weekend or a few days away would be enough. Probably not Scotland, as it's a long way for a weekend, but North Wales or the Lake District were certainly options.

But for now, it was lovely relaxing with a drink beside the river with someone she found easy to talk to and with whom, unlike her family, she could also discuss work and the satisfaction and frustrations of her role.

She smiled at Sujin as he returned to the seat next to her and placed his hand on top of hers. This was a very pleasant way to spend a summer evening.

CHAPTER TWENTY-ONE

Keya slept deeply, but she still felt tired when she woke on Thursday morning. As she lay in bed and watched weak sunlight filter through her bright flamingo pattern curtains, she thought about her evening with Sujin.

How blissful it had been eating, drinking, and talking together beside the River Coln. As if nothing else mattered.

But it did. And her thoughts turned to Daisy and her death.

Although they'd only met once, Keya had liked the young woman and her positive and enterprising outlook. And she'd loved her bread. Such a shame she wouldn't be able to stock it, unless Theo found someone else to run the bakery. But she doubted sorting that out would be a priority for him right now.

And then there was the manner of Daisy's death, with no reasonable explanation for why the young woman had sat down, closed her eyes, and died. So why was she so certain someone else had caused it?

The results of the blood tests, and any other analysis the pathologist was performing, would take time to come through, and what if they were inconclusive? Would the coroner be forced to conclude an open verdict because there was insufficient evidence for anything else?

Perhaps Ryan or Sujin would discover a motive for Daisy's death in her phone calls, emails, or other digital messages.

Keya had interviewed all the people she was aware of who were close to Daisy, and there wasn't anything else she could ask without further information. At least it meant she could spend some time at her cafe.

After showering and dressing, Keya quickly ate a yogurt while she filled her Waterwheel Cafe thermal mug with coffee, and then she drove to the cafe.

It was just after half past eight when she arrived and parked in the main car park in front of the antique centre. The centre's heavy oak front doors were open to allow fresh air to circulate inside.

Keya glanced up. Clouds skidded across the sky, and she wouldn't be surprised if it rained later.

Gilly rushed over when she entered the large open-plan space which was the ground floor of the antique centre. The front row of stalls included several with attractive vintage furnishings, one which sold colourful glassware, and another which only displayed wooden items.

"What news of the dead girl?" Gilly asked, her voice carrying to a woman who was arranging cushions on a ladder stand. The woman dropped a cushion, so Keya suggested, "Come and have a cup of tea."

She and Gilly strode alongside the white painted stone wall which separated the antique centre from the single-storey auction house next door. They passed a group of gilt-framed mirrors hanging from the wall and then some retro metal signs, including a black one advertising Jack Daniel's Whiskey.

Inside the cafe, there was a smell of frying bacon coming from the kitchen. Millie was cleaning tables with a disinfectant spray and a blue and white cloth.

"Oh, that smells good," Gilly said, glancing towards the kitchen hatch.

"Would you like a bacon sandwich?" Keya asked.

"I better not." Gilly tapped her ample tummy, "but I wouldn't say no to a cup of tea."

Gilly leaned against the hot drinks counter as Keya boiled the kettle and prepared their cups of tea. She'd only drunk half her morning coffee, but she now fancied a cup of tea.

"So, have you found out what happened to the girl at the stones?" Gilly asked again.

"We're no further forward than we were when we spoke yesterday," Keya replied. "And I'm not certain we'll ever know what really happened."

Keya slid Gilly's tea across the counter, and as she did so, she felt Gilly staring at her.

"What?" she asked.

"You look tired. Like you need a holiday."

"That's what Sujin said," and when Gilly raised her eyebrows, Keya added, "Not with him. Perhaps with Dotty if she has any time off. Nothing fancy, just a short break in the UK."

"That sounds an excellent idea, but I suggest you go before the school holidays. The prices at least double from the end of July through August."

"Did someone mention holidays?" Monica asked as she approached the counter. "And I'd love a cup of coffee if you're making one. I need something to get me going this morning."

Monica was Ryan's mum. She had the same cheerful demeanour as her son, and a positive outlook on life. She was short and neat, with her dark hair streaked with grey, cut into a bob. Her only extravagance was her shoes. Today she was wearing a pair of baby pink ballet style shoes which Keya was concerned she'd ruin by dropping tomato sauce or hot oil on them.

"Yes, we think Keya needs a break," Gilly said.

"I agree. You're always racing from the cafe to the police station and back again. Where are you thinking of going?" asked Monica eagerly.

"I don't know. It was only a suggestion Sujin made yesterday. About going with Dotty," Keya added hastily.

As she prepared Monica's coffee, her mind wandered back to the previous evening. Sujin was knowledgeable on a wide range of subjects and, when he spoke about them, he made them sound interesting, rather than boring. And her pasta had been perfect. Rich and creamy, and she and Sujin had shared a salad which had added freshness.

And she'd found his hand on hers reassuring rather than possessive.

"Keya, are you listening?" Monica demanded.

"Sorry, what were you saying?"

"That I have lots of brochures for cruises and African safaris. I really can't make up my mind which we should do. A cruise will be relaxing with every luxury provided and we can visit lots of different places. But this might be my last chance to visit Africa and I so want to see elephants and giraffes in the wild."

Keya handed Monica a steaming cup of coffee and said, "That sounds great," although she knew her voice lacked enthusiasm.

But Monica didn't appear to notice. "I know. And I never believed I could afford such a trip until you let me work here. It's all so exciting."

Keya thought she saw in Monica a dutiful wife and mother, who'd finally been allowed her freedom and the chance to earn her own money and spend it as she wanted. Keya smiled, delighted that she'd been able to offer Monica such an opportunity. And Monica was a great cook and a steady head in the kitchen during busy periods of service in the cafe.

"I think I'll only manage a few days away this time. Perhaps to Wales or the Lake District," Keya said.

Monica looked disappointed.

Keya's phone rang, and she looked down at the screen. "It's Ryan."

She stepped out from behind the counter and away from Gilly and Monica as she took the call.

"Morning Ryan. Do you have news of Daisy's death?"

"Afraid not. But Farmer Minchin, on whose land the Rollright Standing Stones are located, made an angry call this morning reporting people vandalising his crops. Apparently, there's a crop circle in the field next to the stones."

Keya groaned.

"Can you pick Warren up from the station and take him with you?"

"Warren?" Keya queried.

"Constable Sparrow."

Keya sighed. Time to get back to her other job. "Tell him to be there in twenty minutes."

CHAPTER TWENTY-TWO

Once again Keya approached the Rollright Standing Stones. This time a pale blue battered Land Rover Defender was parked in the first lay-by.

She pulled up behind it as an angry-looking man with red cheeks and a flat tweed cap climbed out. He waited for her and Warren, his feet planted wide apart, and he did not look happy.

"Mr Minchin?" asked Keya as she pulled her black police hat onto her head and rearranged her ponytail, so it sat snugly.

"Aye, and you'll be t'police."

"Sergeant Varma, and my colleague, Constable Sparrow. You reported an act of vandalism."

"Aye, someone has destroyed my wheat and bashed it down to create a daft pattern. Aurora and her like will tell you it's the spirits, but it ain't. Someone has deliberately damaged my crop."

"I'm sorry to hear that," Keya commiserated as she, Warren and Farmer Minchin entered the grassy area of the standing stones.

The blue and white police tape flapped in the gathering wind.

"It's bad enough folks trampling about at the stones and wandering out into my field, but this is deliberate."

"I understand, sir. This isn't the first crop circle we've been called to this month," Keya explained.

Farmer Minchin led them down a narrow path clear of growing wheat towards the centre of the field. It was hard to tell from ground level the exact shape of the crop circle, but Keya marvelled at the creativeness of whoever had made it.

"See, flattened and lying on the floor. It'll considerably decrease my yield. Make sure you write that in your report."

Keya considered Farmer Minchin. Was he annoyed at the damage caused or more concerned with claiming as much as possible on his insurance?

Warren moved around the area, taking photographs with his phone while Keya asked the obligatory questions.

"So when did you discover the damage?"

"This morning, when I called you lot," replied the red-faced farmer.

"And when did you last check the field?"

"Couple of days ago. Before all the folk turned up for the solstice."

"So this," she indicated with her arm towards the laid wheat crop, "could have been done anytime over the past few days."

"Aye. But it's still ruined my crop."

Keya and Warren left Farmer Minchin and his damaged wheat crop and drove back to the police station.

"How do we solve this crime?" asked Warren from the passenger seat as he looked through the photographs he'd taken of the crop circle.

"With luck, I suspect," sighed Keya. "But the culprit will be forced to stop once the fields are harvested. Someone might spot whoever is creating the designs, but by their very nature, most fields are remote and if the work is done at night, or early in the morning, the likelihood of the creator being seen is low."

Keya slowed to a stop and looked left and right before driving straight over the crossroads. "Vandalism in the countryside has been a concern for years now, but as I'm the only officer officially overseeing the area, there isn't much I can do unless the culprits are caught in the act."

Deciding to change the subject, Keya asked, "Did you find anything useful in the rubbish we brought back from the standing stones yesterday?"

"Inspector Evans suggested I speak to Sujin about it, and he told me he'd set up a sorting area this morning, so I guess I'll get on with it when I return to the station." Warren didn't sound thrilled by the prospect.

When they arrived at the police station, Keya accompanied Warren to Sujin's workroom. She knocked on his closed door, noticing the sound of opera singing coming from inside the workroom.

"Come in," Sujin called, and he turned the volume down as Keya entered. Warren hovered in the doorway.

Noticing him, Sujin announced, "I've set up a table for you. Wear the protective gloves I've left, as we don't want you cutting or stabbing yourself."

"What am I looking for?" asked Warren uncertainly.

"Anything obvious, like a weapon. Put syringes or needles to one side, and any cigarette butts in a pile. Place drinks containers and cups in the blue plastic bin and food containers in the green one. And put to one side anything that you don't think should be there." Sujin smiled at Warren as if he was about to embark on an exciting task.

Warren nodded and moved away from the workroom.

"Now I can say a proper good morning. How are you?" Sujin asked Keya.

"Confounded by mystic crop circles and young women dropping dead for no apparent reason."

Sujin looked away, but not before Keya noticed the disappointment on his face.

"But I enjoyed last night. It was so relaxing sitting by the river, and the food was lovely too." She wondered if she should have added, and so was the company, but she suddenly felt awkward and self-conscious.

Sujin looked up and smiled softly at her before suggesting, "Perhaps we can do it again. Soon."

Keya nodded. "I'd like that." Then she spotted the phone lying on Sujin's worktable with Daisy's phone case next to it. Back to business.

"Have you managed to access Daisy's phone?" she asked.

Sujin gave her a lingering look before taking a deep breath and turning back to his worktable. "Yes. I charged it overnight and unlocked it earlier this morning. I emailed you and your team a list of phone calls and messages, but I know you also like paper copies." He handed Keya some stapled sheets of paper.

"Did anything jump out at you?" Keya asked.

Sujin considered the question before replying. "People always wanted something from her. For her to do this or that, but very few messages were from those who were helping or doing something for Daisy. Apart from Theo. He'd send little messages or memes of love, and he was the only one who ever asked how she was feeling."

"You don't think he killed her, do you?" Keya said.

"Not from what I've seen, but her phone is only one piece of evidence. And I haven't actually met him in person."

Keya was about to leave when she remembered the photos she'd transferred from Gilly's phone.

"Oh! I have the photos Gilly Wimsey took before I arrived yesterday morning. Can I transfer them to you?"

Once the task was complete, Sujin uploaded the photos and displayed them on his computer monitor.

Keya leaned closer as she examined them.

"That's Aurora and Viv. And the two sisters with the baby, and the ladies from Durham. Um." On several photographs of the standing stones and the area around where Daisy's body had been discovered, there was a young man loitering. He was wearing all black, apart from a pale green T-shirt, and had a shaven head.

She pointed at one image of the young man and said, "I met him in Daisy's bakery, although I've now forgotten his name."

"Could it be Ash?" Sujin suggested.

As Keya turned to him, she realised how close they were. Staring into his eyes, she asked, her voice catching in her throat, "Why?"

Sujin smiled and then looked down at Daisy's phone. "Because there were lots of messages from him. I think he works for the bakery or the mill as there were messages asking about collection, deliveries, and supplies, but there were also personal ones. The most recent were quite desperate, even threatening, demanding to know what Daisy saw in Theo, and telling her Theo was too old for her."

"Do you think there's some history there?"

"I do," Sujin confirmed.

Keya returned to the team room, passing Warren, who was

standing beside a white plastic table now covered in an assortment of rubbish. He picked up a drink can and dropped it into a blue plastic bin next to the table.

She smiled as she entered the team room, pleased she no longer had to perform such tasks.

"Something amusing?" asked Inspector Evans in a flat voice.

"Not really," Keya replied, composing her expression. "And certainly not in Farmer Minchin's field."

"It's quite spectacular, though," said Ryan, looking up from his computer.

"What is?" asked Keya, turning towards him.

"His crop circle. Someone photographed it from a drone. Come and have a look. It's star shaped with points and little circular balls, as well as the expected concentric circles."

Keya squeezed between Ryan and Sujin's old desk and peered at Ryan's screen. "Wow, that must have taken ages. How did someone manage to create all that in one night? And if they didn't do it last night, how did they do it without being spotted by people attending the solstice?"

"But that's the point. What if the spirits created it in memory of Daisy?" Ryan looked at her, his eyes wide but with a twinkle in them.

Keya drew her lips together.

Ryan added quickly, "That's what the social media posts are saying, anyway."

Keya groaned and sloped back to her desk. She'd just collapsed onto her chair when Stan arrived carrying a tray of hot drinks.

Keya eyed him gratefully. "A cup of tea is just what I need."

CHAPTER TWENTY-THREE

Keya sipped her tea as she examined the stapled sheets of messages and phone calls logged from Daisy's phone.

Using a pencil, she circled the calls to and from Ash. Ash made considerably more calls to Daisy than she made to him.

And then there were the messages. Keya started from as far back as they went, which was two years. They started with words of concern and support for Daisy and read like two close friends corresponding.

Then there must have been the time when Daisy and her father fell out as the messages were more urgent and Ashley insisted he could help. They turned from desperate to angry at the period Keya judged Daisy had moved out and into Mill House.

They included such phrases as, 'Why go to him?' and 'I can look after you best'.

For a time, the messages had stopped, or Daisy had deleted them, and then they'd started up again, but Daisy's tone had changed and was more impersonal. That was at the same time as the business-related messages had started.

Keya judged that the relationship between Ash and Daisy was civil before her death but strained, particularly on Ash's side, but it was hard to tell because of the shorthand he used.

Keya finished her tea and sat back as Inspector Evans appeared in his office doorway. He asked, "What are your plans for today?"

"I think I'll interview Ash, the young man I met in Daisy's bakery. They've been messaging each other for a while and he clearly had a thing for her, and he wasn't happy when she moved in with Theo."

"Very good." The inspector turned to Ryan and asked, "Constable Jenkins?"

"I'm working through Daisy's emails, and then I'll check her phone calls from the list Sujin sent over after unlocking her phone. I'm still waiting to hear back from her bank."

"Let me know at lunchtime if you're still waiting and I'll contact them myself," instructed the inspector.

This time, Keya drove directly to the Stone Circle Flour mill. Opposite the main mill buildings was a low single-storey stone building, painted white. She parked in front of it and entered the door marked reception.

A bell tinkled, and a voice called, "I'll be with you in a minute."

Several minutes later, a young man wearing a grey Stone Circle Flour polo shirt and black chino trousers emerged from a side office and said, "Sorry to keep you waiting, Officer. But if you want to speak to Mr Watson, he's at home." The young man leaned forward and lowered his voice. "He's taking a few days' compassionate leave, and who can blame him? Terrible business. We all loved Daisy."

Which seemed to be the consensus wherever Keya went.

"Actually, I'm looking for one of your delivery drivers. Ash."

"Oh," the young man replied.

"Is that a problem?"

The man leaned further forward, and Keya stepped closer as he confided, "You mean Ashley Ricketts? He had a thing for Daisy. Apparently, they were childhood sweethearts, so he wasn't happy when she moved in with Mr Watson. One evening, after I think he'd had a little too much to drink at the Malt Shovel, he stood outside Mill House and serenaded Daisy. But when Theo shouted at him to go away, he turned abusive. Quite the language he knew, if you get my drift."

The young man raised his eyebrows before adding, "It was actually Daisy's mum, Mrs Skinner, who persuaded him to leave."

"But Ashley still works at the mill?"

"Yes. I think Mr Watson wanted to get rid of him, although he's a very reliable delivery driver, but I suspect Daisy persuaded him not to. She was like that. Kind, considerate, and she stood up for the little people."

Keya wondered if this young man considered himself to be one of the 'little people'.

"Where can I find Ashley?" Keya asked.

The young man moved behind a desk and tapped a keyboard as he looked at a computer screen.

"He came back twenty minutes ago and is due out again in twenty-five. Shall I call him over?"

"Yes, please," Keya replied.

The young man picked up a device and spoke into it.

Keya heard his voice echo outside.

"Please take a seat," said the man. "And can I bring you a tea, coffee, or perhaps a glass of water?"

"A tea, please. And is there somewhere private I can speak to Ashley?"

"You can stay here. I have some work to do in Mr Watson's office, but you can call me if you need anything."

A few minutes later, the shaven headed figure of Ashley entered the office. He was dressed in black jeans and a light-blue Stone Circle Flour T-shirt.

"You want ..." He broke off when he saw Keya sitting on a grey reception chair. "I suppose you want to talk to me about Daisy? I didn't kill her, if that's what you think. I would never harm Daisy. I loved her."

"Come and sit down, Mr Ricketts."

"Call me Ash. Everyone else does."

"OK, Ash. As you've deduced, I'm here to talk to you about Daisy. I take it the two of you have been friends for a long time."

"For ever. We're the same age so we were in the same year at school, and we used to catch the school bus together to Chipping Norton. We've always been friends."

"But you wanted something more than friendship?" Keya suggested.

"Of course. We were going to get married and have children and live in a little cottage. That's what we'd talked about since we were young."

"But then Theo arrived, and all that changed?"

"Yeah. And how could I compete with the new mill manager? One of Sir Anthony's relations."

"How did you feel when Daisy's father threw her out and she moved into Mill House?"

"I felt sorry for Daisy. Mr Bentham always made her do all the jobs around the house, and he even had her working on his business. That's why she wouldn't come away with me to work in London."

"You had a job in London?"

"Yeah. For an insurance company. I'm good with computers. But Daisy wouldn't leave her father and her sister. So we both stayed."

Keya clarified, "So you stayed here and gave up your future career for Daisy?"

"Yeah. We said we'd always be together."

Keya wondered at the simplicity of Ash's love for Daisy. "So you must have felt let down and hurt when Daisy moved into Mill House."

"I did, but I understood. She had nowhere else to go. And she could hardly move in with my mam, brother, and me. We're cramped enough as it is."

"But you thought it was only temporary?"

Ash pursed his lips together. "Yeah. But then Theo told me to stop calling round to visit Daisy. He said she didn't want to see me, which I knew was a lie. Daisy wouldn't do that."

Keya wasn't so sure. She could believe Theo wanting to put a stop to Ash's visits, but he might have done so at Daisy's request if she didn't want to hurt Ash's feelings. Whichever was correct, Ash was clearly on the wrong side of the love triangle.

"Did you ever threaten Daisy?"

"Don't be daft," Ash responded easily. "Why would I do that?"

"And Theo?"

Ash inclined his head.

"Have you ever threatened Theo Watson?"
"I might have done," Ash muttered. "But I didn't mean to."
Keya didn't believe him.

CHAPTER TWENTY-FOUR

Keya didn't find out anything else of use from Ash, who insisted he loved Daisy and would never harm her. However, it was clear that he wasn't beyond violence where Theo Watson was concerned.

The interview was terminated when the young man came out of the side office and said, "Ashley. Your truck is full. You need to start your delivery round."

Ash jumped up and was out of the door before Keya had a chance to thank him for his time. She did thank the young man for her tea before leaving the reception area.

Back to the station, she thought, after a rather unsatisfactory interview.

Her phone buzzed, and she checked her messages.

Ryan had sent one.

Please can you collect Theo Watson's phone?

She could certainly try. Returning to her car, she drove to Mill House.

There was no answer when she rapped the black wheatsheaf knocker against the front door. But finding the door unlocked, she opened it slowly, calling, "Theo? It's Sergeant Varma. Are you OK?"

There was no response, so she cautiously entered the property, praying she wouldn't find another dead body.

But Theo was alive, if not well, curled up on a sofa in the living room. The curtains were still drawn, so Keya pulled them open, allowing weak sunlight to illuminate the room.

Theo was pale and wearing the same clothes as the previous day. Keya thought he'd probably slept on the sofa.

"Theo, I know you're hurting, but you won't be able to help Daisy, or help us find out what happened to her, in this state."

Theo finally focused his eyes on Keya.

"Officer?"

"Sergeant Varma. But you can call me Keya."

"Keya," Theo repeated in a dream-like voice.

"Now what I want you to do is go upstairs and shower, and put on a clean set of clothes while I make you something to eat."

Theo stared at her uncertainly.

"Upstairs," she instructed more firmly.

Theo uncurled his legs and placed his bare feet on the Indian rug covering the floor. Hesitantly, he stood up muttering, "Shower," before he wandered out of the room and up the stairs.

Keya checked her watch. It was a quarter past twelve. Nearly lunchtime.

She found eggs in an attractive pottery chicken on the sideboard, and ham, mushrooms, tomatoes, and cheese in the fridge. She'd make omelettes and use some of the mixed lettuce leaves and radishes also in the fridge to create a side salad. There were also attractive and fragrant pots of herbs on the windowsill above the double stainless-steel sink.

She was happily frying a second omelette when Theo appeared in the kitchen. He hadn't shaved, but his hair was damp, and he was wearing a clean pair of jeans and a green T-shirt with a daisy on the front. On his bare feet were a pair of suede slippers.

"Grab yourself a knife and fork and sit down." Keya placed his plate down on the table. The omelette was a deep yellow colour from what she presumed were free range eggs. "Help yourself to salad and I've found a range of condiments."

Next to the salad, Keya had arranged containers of tomato ketchup, mayonnaise, a tall bottle with an orange label with 'hot sauce' printed on it, and a jar of homemade tomato chutney.

Keya finished cooking her omelette and slid it onto a plate. She sat down opposite Theo.

He picked up the hot sauce, studied it, and then placed it back on the table. "Daisy brought that out when she cooked Mexican dishes, although she only occasionally had any. But she pretended she liked it, as her mum made it. It's good, but too spicy for today." He reached for the tomato chutney.

"I might try some." Keya poured a little of the hot sauce onto her plate. It was spicy, and it certainly gave her vegetable omelette a kick.

She and Theo sat in silence, as she wanted him to concentrate on his food and make sure he ate it before she started asking any questions.

They finished their omelettes, and Keya handed Theo an individual pot of chocolate mousse she'd also found in the fridge.

As she peeled the foil cover off her own pot, she said, "I spoke to Ashley Ricketts this morning. He's not a fan of yours."

"I know. But then he and Daisy have been friends for years and I know he thought they'd have the fairy tale white wedding and live happily ever after. He sees me as the evil ogre, so to speak, who spoiled his fantasy. But that's all it was. A girl like Daisy was never going to settle for someone like Ash."

"But he was the one with plans for moving to London."

"Was he? I didn't know about that. It would have solved all our problems."

Keya let the comment pass and considered, "I think it was before you came along. But Daisy refused to leave her father and sister."

Theo dipped a teaspoon into his chocolate mousse. "Now that I can understand. Dennis had Daisy caught in a trap. I'm not sure she'd ever have got out if I hadn't arrived in the village. I didn't mean to cause the row which led to Dennis throwing Daisy out, but I'm not sorry I did. That's when she was finally free of him."

But did Daisy feel beholden to her knight in shining armour, Keya wondered.

"Didn't Daisy resent you, even a little bit, for that?"

"She was certainly upset at first. There were lots of tears. But when they subsided, it was Zoe she was most concerned about. She asked me if her sister could live with us. I didn't have a problem with it. We have plenty of room. But by then, Dennis had his claws into Zoe, just as he had done with Daisy. But Daisy hadn't given up hope and was still trying to persuade Zoe to move in here."

"And what about Daisy's mum?" Keya enquired.

"Doreen? What about her?"

"What was her relationship like with Daisy? Had they had an argument?"

"Not that I'm aware of, but I guess you could say their relationship was a tricky one. I'm not sure Daisy completely forgave her mum for running out on her and Zoe. They were civil, and deep down, I know they both cared for each other. But Daisy moving in here and setting up the bakery, and blossoming into an attractive young woman with prospects… I'd say Doreen was bitter about it. But that isn't unusual with mother-daughter relationships, is it?"

Keya thought of her own family. Her mother certainly wasn't jealous of her job, and she'd helped Keya when she started the cafe, but what her mother wanted most was for Keya to marry and produce grandchildren. It sounded very different from the relationship between Daisy and her mother.

"And how do you get on with Doreen? You're her boss, aren't you?"

"Yes, but she started working at the mill before I arrived. I think my uncle felt sorry for her, but she's a hard worker and I have no issue with her. In fact, one of our supervisors is retiring in the autumn, and I'm considering Doreen for the position. She's capable of taking on the role if her self-confidence will allow her to step up and do it."

Keya hadn't thought of Doreen as someone who lacked self-confidence, but she could certainly see her as a hard worker.

"And what about everyone else in the village? Dora appeared upset about Daisy's plans for Mill House."

"Is she? She's always been supportive of them in front of me. But I know she wasn't happy when she and her father moved out. Uncle Anthony said they could stay, and I'd have been happy with a cottage in the village, but Uncle Thomas, Dora's father, was insistent.

He said it was time to move on and make way for the new manager. Me."

That wasn't how Dora had told it.

"And Dr and Mrs Reid?"

"Harmless. Mrs Reid was annoyed when we opened the bakery, but I've seen her sneak in for bread and cakes. And Dr Reid is more concerned about the ancient world, and the standing stones, and archaeology. He's a bit stuffy and gets annoyed when the mill is working overtime, but he always gets over it."

"And Aurora and Viv?"

"They're good fun, if a bit wacky. But I know Daisy was worried about their influence over Zoe. But at least they were getting her away from Dennis."

Keya checked her black wristwatch. "I should be getting back to the station."

"Thank you so much for lunch and the chat," Theo said, in a grateful voice. "I feel better about it. I might even wander down to the office. Sitting here on my own is doing me no good whatsoever. And I know Daisy wouldn't want me falling apart and letting the business and everything we've worked for suffer."

"What about the bakery?" asked Keya tentatively.

"I'm not sure. I need to think about it."

"There is one more thing. I'm afraid I need to take your phone back to the station with me?"

"What for?" Theo looked perplexed rather than annoyed.

"Our forensic team needs to check it alongside Daisy's. It shouldn't take more than a couple of days, if that."

"Was there something on Daisy's phone? Was she receiving hate messages?" Theo asked, in a concerned voice.

"No, nothing like that. Although I think there may be some messages from Ashley which she deleted."

Theo winced. "I remember those. Soon after she moved in here. He bombarded her with them. He was concerned about her at first, but then he turned abusive. She blocked his messages, so he turned up in person, drunk. I told him to go away and his anger turned on me, but I was fine with that. After all, I was his boss and if he wanted to keep his job, he had to be civil. Things settled down after a few months."

Theo left the kitchen and returned a minute later carrying his phone. As he handed it to Keya, he said, "Keep it for as long as you like if it will help determine what happened to Daisy. I'll use a work one. But please be careful and make sure you don't delete any of the photos. I'll need them to help me get through the next few weeks and months."

CHAPTER TWENTY-FIVE

When Keya returned to her team room in the police station, she found Ryan with Inspector Evans in his small office.

"Monday is not good enough," she heard Inspector Evans bluster.

Thinking he was annoyed with Ryan, Keya poked her head into the inspector's office. Ryan gave her a wry smile as Inspector Evans said into his phone, "This is a potential murder investigation. We need Daisy Bentham's bank details today."

He slammed the phone down as Keya ducked out of the office, but she was too late.

"Sergeant. You've been a long time."

"Yes, sir," she replied as she stepped back into the inspector's office. "I met with Ashley Ricketts, the young man who had a thing for Daisy. He certainly has a temper, but would he harm Daisy? I doubt it. And if he did, he'd do so in a more obvious way. If there is a crime, I think it's too sophisticated for him."

"OK. But don't rule him out yet. A scorned lover and all that," the inspector remarked.

"And talking of lovers, I went to Mill House to collect Theo Watson's phone."

"Did you get it?" asked Ryan hopefully.

"I did, and I had a good chat with Theo, which is why it took me so long. He was in a terrible state, so I made him shower while I cooked lunch."

Inspector Evans raised his eyebrows, but he refrained from saying anything.

"Just omelettes," she clarified quickly. "He relaxed as we ate, and we discussed Daisy and his relationships with her family and people in the village."

"And is there anyone who held a grudge against our victim?" the inspector enquired.

"Not that Theo was aware of." Keya held out Theo's phone for Ryan to take.

"Actually," Ryan said, "you should give it to Sujin first. He'll give it to me when he's finished with it."

Keya left the inspector's office and walked down the corridor to the custody suite. The white plastic table where Warren had been working had been cleared away, although the green and blue plastic bins were still beside the wall.

Keya knocked on Sujin's door, wondering why she couldn't hear any music.

"Come in," Sujin called, but when she opened the door there was hardly any room for her inside.

Warren was standing next to Sujin and together they were examining the end of a hand-rolled cigarette.

"Keya, come in. Warren is helping me establish if anything Daisy ate, drank, or inhaled killed her. We've come up negative with the can of cider which had her fingerprints and saliva on it, so we're now checking this homemade cigarette."

Sujin picked it up with a pair of forceps and sniffed it.

"Definitely herbal. I'll need to conduct more tests to find out exactly what it contains. And, of course, we need the results of the saliva test to confirm Daisy sucked it."

Keya placed Theo's phone on a clear area of workspace near the door. "Ryan asked me to give you Theo's phone to examine. Can you give it to him when you've finished with it?"

"OK. Thanks." Sujin placed the cigarette back on the worktable and reached for a scalpel.

"Did you find anything else of interest in the rubbish?" Keya asked.

"Not that immediately stood out," Sujin replied, concentrating on cutting the cigarette.

Keya decided to leave him to his work and returned to the team room. As she sat down at her desk to write up her notes, her phone rang.

It was Gilly. "Are you coming back to the cafe this afternoon?" she asked.

"I can do," Keya replied.

"Great. I want to sit down and discuss the open-air cinema night. Will five o'clock be OK?"

Keya checked her watch. It was just after three.

"Sure. I'll be there."

Keya started to write up her notes.

Ryan looked up from the opposite desk and asked, "Any ideas for what I can do with the cadets tonight?"

Inspector Evans stepped out of his office and asked, "Your turn to be in charge of the Volunteer Cadet Force, is it, Constable?"

"Yes, sir."

"Then why don't we make it realistic and give them a summary of the case we're currently working on? See what ideas they have, as I'm certainly struggling to understand what happened."

"We, sir?" Ryan queried.

"Do you have any objection to me talking to them?"

"Certainly not, sir. I just thought you'd want to go home and ..." Ryan's voice trailed off.

"Stare at the walls?" asked the inspector, raising his eyebrows. "I do enough of that already."

"And you could ask them what they know about crop circles?" Keya suggested.

"There you are, Constable Jenkins. A full itinerary. Now you better make some slides or something you can hand round explaining what we've done so far in the case."

Keya finished her notes and, not envying Ryan his task, or having the assistance of Inspector Evans at the evening's cadets' meeting, she said, "I'm needed at the cafe. I'll see you all in the morning."

As she passed Ryan's desk, she mouthed, "Good luck."

CHAPTER TWENTY-SIX

Keya parked round the side of the cafe, in the new car park, and walked towards the deli. The weather was still warm, despite the clouds and the wind. She watched as her youngest sister scooped chocolate ice cream onto a cone for a young girl.

The girl happily skipped away as Keya joined Maitri and said, "Your idea for the ice cream cart is popular."

"Yes, and it's only June. Hopefully, we'll have lots more customers in the school holidays, but it'll depend on the weather." She looked up at the clouds and frowned. "And I suppose we won't be getting our fresh bread order now?"

"I spoke to Theo today, and he'd like to keep the bakery going, but it isn't a priority."

"That's a shame. But come and try these pickles that a local farmer's wife brought in."

Inside the deli, there were metal racks displaying an assortment of items, from gluten-free pasta, to flavoured mayonnaise, and handmade luxury biscuits. Fridges and freezers against one wall contained meats, ready meals, and a selection of frozen berries.

Maitri stepped behind the counter, part of which was chilled and displayed sliced meats, cheeses and ready-prepared salads. The salads were Maitri's latest idea, and she arrived early each morning to prepare a selection with Monica and their new kitchen assistant, Mick.

Maitri handed Keya a savoury biscuit topped with a lumpy yellow mixture.

"Piccalilli. That's the spicy version."

It certainly was. Keya bit a piece of carrot in the piccalilli and gasped for air.

"The vegetables are perfect," she said. "With just the right crunch, but that's too hot even for me!"

Maitri laughed and handed Keya a glass of water.

After drinking half of it, Keya said, "I know piccalilli should have a sharp vinegar and mustard taste, but I think that's too much."

"Try this one," suggested Maitri, handing Keya another loaded biscuit.

"Perfect," said Keya, swallowing the fruity, spicy mixture. "I know Norman would enjoy that with a slice of cold ham. Anything else?"

Keya tasted a range of chutneys and they agreed they'd stock all but the plum chutney and the spicy piccalilli.

When she and Maitri had finished their tasting and discussion of other items to stock, including Maitri's suggestion of ready-prepared sandwiches for customers on the go, Keya left the deli and entered the cafe.

It was still a third full, even though it was after four o'clock.

Norman signalled to her from his hot drinks counter, making a T-sign with his hands, and she nodded her acceptance.

Millie was seating an elderly couple and Alison, who'd started working in the cafe the previous month, was serving scones and cakes to three well-dressed ladies. Everything appeared calm and under control.

Together, Millie and Alison had taken over most of the restocking, which was a huge relief to Keya and saved her from rushing to and from the cash and carry. But as she stood watching her employees going about their business, she felt isolated.

Opening a small cafe and deli had been her dream, but at the moment she wasn't able to live it. She couldn't complain. The cafe was proving popular, and Maitri was making a real success of the deli, but what was her part in it all?

Glancing towards the kitchen hatch, she saw Mick's tattooed arm place a toasted panini on a plate beside a small salad and bowls of crisps and coleslaw. Since he'd been released from prison, acquitted of a crime he hadn't committed, he'd taken well to his work in the kitchen. And that was where Keya would like to be. Not all the time, but at least part of the week, baking and creating dishes for customers to enjoy.

Norman signalled to her as he placed her cup of tea on the counter.

When she approached him, he asked, "What's bothering you?"

There was no point hiding her feelings, so she said, "I don't feel part of this anymore. Don't get me wrong, I'm delighted with how well the cafe is doing, and I'm grateful for everyone's help, but I hardly get to spend any time here."

"That's because you're out there ensuring justice is served. And not everyone can do that," replied Norman, seriously. "People rely on you to find out what happened. I presume you're currently working on the death of the young woman up at the standing stones."

"Yes, we are." Keya sipped her tea.

"It's important for her loved ones to know how she died. And if it was foul play, to bring the culprit to justice. The cafe's not going away. Look at how much you've achieved in just a year."

Keya smiled gratefully and corrected, "How much WE'VE achieved."

"Watch out," Norman warned, lowering his voice. "Here comes Beanie."

Keya sipped her tea again as she watched the flamboyant figure of Aunt Beanie sail across the cafe. She waved at the elderly couple who'd recently arrived before reaching the drinks counter.

Dotty, who was following Aunt Beanie, stopped to talk to Millie. They both laughed before also heading towards the hot drinks counter.

"Two cappuccinos," Millie ordered before moving on to the kitchen hatch.

"Fabulous, you're here, Keya. I've brought Dotty with me so we can discuss plans for Gilly's birthday before she arrives to talk about the open-air cinema.'

"You have spoken to Dr Peter, haven't you?" Norman asked in a warning tone.

"Of course," Aunt Beanie replied contritely. "We've agreed to hold the party on her birthday. It's a Thursday, so that should be OK for most people. And we thought an evening event at the cafe would work best." Aunt Beanie turned to Keya and smiled in satisfaction.

Keya, who had raised her cup to her lips, stared at the older woman.

"I told you we should have asked Keya first," Dotty said, before smiling apologetically at her friend.

"A party. Here?" Keya questioned.

"Yes. It's the perfect venue. We can move the tables around to create space for guests to stand and mingle when they arrive, and then we can serve food from the kitchen. Depending on the weather, people can sit inside or outside and the band ..."

"What band?" Keya interjected.

"Why, your friend Sujin's Celtic Twisters. They're not cheap, but Millie assured me they're very good."

Keya felt her head spin. Not only did she no longer feel part of her cafe, but she was struggling to keep up with her own life.

"Can we sit down?" she suggested. "And walk me through it."

"Of course," Aunt Beanie replied, pulling out a chair at a neighbouring table. "And a pot of tea for Dotty and me when you're ready, Norman."

Norman rolled his eyes and turned his back as he frothed up milk for the customers' cappuccinos.

"So it's Gilly's birthday this month?" Keya asked.

"Yes, I told you," Aunt Beanie replied in an exasperated tone. "It's her big five O. And she's having all sorts of reactions to it. One minute she's moaning about being old and the next she's twittering on about being free and living the second half of her life with nature."

Dotty smiled.

Which made Keya relax, and she also grinned at her imaginary image of a barefoot Gilly dancing in a meadow with songbirds circling her head.

"It's serious. You young folk don't know what it's like to grow old."

Dotty and Keya both composed themselves and Keya asked, "So you thought of throwing a party for Gilly, here, at the cafe?"

"Yes," Aunt Beanie insisted. "It's the ideal venue."

Keya leaned back in her chair and looked around. Aunt Beanie had a point. If they pushed the tables and chairs together, they could create an area for people to stand and chat when they arrived and the band …

"Have you booked the Celtic Twisters?"

"Yes, last night. They have a weekend festival, so they said they can only perform for a couple of hours, but I'm sure that will be fine. We won't want to be too late after all."

Keya wondered why Sujin hadn't mentioned anything to her.

"So is that OK? Dotty said she'd help and liaise with Monica and Millie if you're busy."

"I don't want to interfere," Dotty added quickly. "But I don't want you to feel the party is a burden."

Keya paused and took a deep breath. Then she said, "I hope we'll have concluded the current case by then. We've got two weeks, haven't we?"

"Yes, two weeks today."

"What's two weeks today?" asked Gilly, as she joined them.

"My first assessment," Dotty replied quickly.

Keya peered at her friend. It wasn't like her to lie so easily.

Dotty continued, "I hope it won't be too technical, but we have been learning a lot of legal stuff."

"Rather you than me," said Gilly, pulling out the fourth chair and sitting down.

Millie arrived carrying a tray, and she placed cups and a teapot on the table. "Shall I get you two extra cups?"

Keya looked at her empty teacup before replying, "Yes, please."

"So," Gilly began. "The outdoor cinema evening. We've agreed on showing *The Greatest Showman* with sing-along subtitles."

Aunt Beanie clapped her hands together and exclaimed, "Oh, what fun!"

CHAPTER TWENTY-SEVEN

Keya was the first member of her team to arrive at Cirencester Police Station on Friday morning.

She sat down at her desk and checked her messages. No more crop circles. That was a relief.

The following week she was handing out prizes at Shipton-under-Wychwood primary school's sports day, and she had a meeting on Thursday morning to advise on security and policing arrangements for 'The Big Feastival', a local music and food festival.

It had grown into the largest of several music festivals, gaining popularity in the Cotswolds during the summer months, and was held annually on a farm near Kingham, in the north of the area. But more visitors meant more issues, from sunstroke, to drug and alcohol abuse, and violent disputes, particularly amongst the people who camped at the venue.

Next, she checked Daisy's electronic case files and reread all her interview notes to see if there was anything she'd missed, or any points which felt out of place or didn't ring true. There was nothing she could put her finger on.

She could speak to Daisy's father, Dennis, again, as his interview had been extremely short, but what else could she learn from him? She needed to know how Daisy died before she could ask further questions.

She checked the post-mortem file. There was no update, and no blood test results.

Next, she checked Sujin's forensic folder. She was starting to read about the results of the contents of the hand-rolled herbal cigarette when Sujin walked into the office.

"We're playing at your cafe in a couple of weeks for your friend Gilly Wimsey's birthday party. But why didn't you ask me about the band performing?"

Keya looked up and said, "I was going to ask you why you hadn't told me your band will be performing, so I suppose we've both been kept out of the loop. And I think the party's a surprise, so don't mention anything if Gilly is around."

Keya sat back and looked at Sujin. She said, "I was railroaded into the event last night by Aunt Beanie, but now I've thought it over, it should be fun. The cafe is a great venue for a party and if this is a success, perhaps we can do more music evenings."

"It would be fantastic to have another regular venue," Sujin enthused. "We have a few monthly commitments and they're gaining a real following."

"We're also holding a *Greatest Showman* sing-along open-air cinema event at the beginning of July if you're interested?"

"Are you inviting me?" There was a twinkle in Sujin's eyes.

"Yes, but not on a date or anything."

Sujin's face fell.

"What I mean is that I'll be working, and so will Millie, but it doesn't mean we can't spend some time with you and Ryan." Realising that sounded like a double date, she quickly added, "And with Dotty."

Sujin inclined his head to one side and said slowly, "OK. Let me know the date and I'll check if the band has any commitments."

Keya wasn't sure why, but her stomach clenched, and she felt as if she'd missed something. Why was she shying away from spending more time with Sujin? Especially after the lovely evening they'd spent together.

Quickly moving on, she said, "I was checking your notes on that cigarette you tested yesterday. I take it you found Daisy's DNA on it?"

"Yes, hers and several others. Now its contents are interesting and that's what I wanted to discuss with you."

Sujin approached Keya's desk, and she felt more comfortable now they were discussing work again.

"Two components of the herbal mixture are ginseng and aconite," Sujin began.

"Which means what?"

"Ginseng is a common herbal remedy and has many positive effects including being an antioxidant and improving mental and physical activity for people who feel tired. But some people do suffer from negative effects from taking it, including headaches, insomnia, blood pressure fluctuations and rapid heartbeat," Sujin explained.

"Do you think it could have killed Daisy?"

"Not from the little she consumed, but it could be a contributing factor. And then there's aconite."

"Isn't that a poison?"

"It is."

Ryan entered the room and slid quietly behind his desk as Sujin continued, "But some people take it to combat asthma, inflammation, or high blood pressure. Its side effects are severe and include nausea, vomiting, breathing difficulties, heart problems, and ultimately death."

Keya considered what Sujin had told her. Nobody had mentioned Daisy vomiting, but she had felt the need to sit down. Had she suffered any more side effects? And had others smoked similar cigarettes? There hadn't been reports of anyone else being seriously ill.

"But why Daisy? Not anyone else?" she asked out loud.

"Her cigarette could have contained more aconite than the ones other people smoked. Or she could have smoked others. One of my jobs today is to examine all the cigarette butts Warren separated from the main rubbish." Sujin sounded dissatisfied.

"But you're not certain this is the cause of death, are you?" Keya asked.

"I'm not saying it isn't, and I've asked the lab to test specifically for aconite in her blood, but it just doesn't sit well with me. I know that's not very scientific," he apologised.

"We're strong on gut feeling in this team," Keya encouraged him. "So if not the cigarette, what else?"

"That's it. I'm fresh out of ideas. It's so frustrating." Sujin pushed his black-framed glasses up his nose.

"It's not your fault," Keya commiserated. "You can't manufacture a reason. Just as I can't make people tell me if they killed her. I've been through all the witness statements, and I've drawn a blank. I can't find a single person who wanted Daisy dead."

Silence filled the room and Sujin shuffled from one foot to another.

Ryan smiled and asked, "Do you want to know how the Volunteer Police Cadets went last night?"

"Yes," Keya and Sujin chorused. Laughing, they looked at each other and Keya suddenly felt the world right itself.

"The inspector was surprisingly good," Ryan started enthusiastically.

"Surprisingly?" echoed Inspector Evans as he entered the room.

Ryan's cheeks flushed. "What I meant, sir, is that I thought you'd be speaking at too high a level for the cadets to understand, but you explained everything clearly and simply to them. And they loved throwing out suggestions as to what could have killed Daisy."

"I don't think it was the midsummer fairies, or that she was abducted by aliens while they created the crop circle, though," remarked the inspector.

"No, but the consensus was poisoning, which seems logical."

"I agree," Sujin said. "Did they make any suggestions with what?"

"Aconite, arsenic, strychnine, bleach, botulinum, food poisoning. Take your pick."

"Great suggestions. They've clearly been doing their research, and their homework. Sergeant Varma and I were just discussing aconite and traces were found in a herbal cigarette we know Daisy smoked. I've asked the lab to test for it, but I doubt there was enough to kill her."

"Did you find anything interesting in the photos Gilly took before I arrived at the standing stones?" Keya asked.

"There were lots more people around than when I arrived with the coroner's ambulance, but they were all keeping their distance from Daisy's body. A couple of shots from the evening before caught Daisy dancing around the fire, but she was very much alive then. And I didn't see anyone slip her anything or arguing with her, if that's what you'd hoped for."

"What else do we have to work on?" Inspector Evans asked.

"I'm going to test the other cigarette ends found at the standing stones," Sujin replied.

"I'll work though Daisy's financial records, which finally arrived yesterday evening," Ryan said.

Keya shrugged her shoulders.

Ryan cleared his throat and suggested, "Perhaps Sergeant Varma can continue looking through Daisy's and Theo's phone records and messages."

"Very good," said Inspector Evans. "Everyone get to work."

CHAPTER TWENTY-EIGHT

Keya spent a dull morning working through Daisy's and Theo's phone records. Warren arrived to help her halfway through the morning, but it was still slow going.

Theo's calls and messages were mostly about work. Doreen had made several complaints about a leaking kitchen roof and blocked drains during May's wet weather, but Theo had answered them politely and helpfully and said he'd send someone round to look at the issues.

Theo had little correspondence with Ash and any that he did have was short, to the point, and work related. On the other hand, Ash's messages to Daisy had become longer and bolder during the past few weeks and it was clear he was trying to entice her away from Theo.

"This is interesting," Keya said to Warren. "About a week ago, after some particularly insistent messages from Ashley to Daisy, she sent him this one. 'Enough. I am not your girl. I am with Theo now and we are planning our future. And our family.'"

"How did Ash respond to that?" Warren asked.

"He didn't. There were no more messages for several days and then there was one asking where to deliver some bread."

Ten minutes later, Keya was scrolling through messages between

Daisy and Doreen which were generally polite, if not particularly affectionate.

"I wonder if Daisy told her mum about her plans to start a family as there's a message from Doreen saying, 'We need to discuss your plans.'"

"But that could mean anything," reasoned Warren.

"You're right." Keya put her section of printed sheets down on her desk and said, "I need a break. And something to eat."

"Sujin suggested we try the new lunchtime menu at The Twelve Bells pub. And there's a nice garden we can sit in," said Ryan.

"I haven't been there for ages. It's run by a local husband and wife team, isn't it?"

"Yes, Carol and Steve. Shall I call Sujin and see if he's ready for lunch?"

While Ryan made the call, Warren asked, "Can I join you?"

"Of course you can. You're part of the team now."

Even Stan abandoned his missus' homemade sandwiches and joined them in the colourful garden at the rear of The Twelve Bells pub. Sujin, Ryan, and Warren carried drinks across to the wooden picnic table where Stan and Keya were sitting.

"Here you go Stan, half a pint of the guest ale." Ryan placed a glass of foamy dark brown liquid in front of Stan and sat down next to him.

"And sparkling water with ice for you, Keya. And Carol added a slice of lemon and a sprig of mint to freshen it up," Sujin said, placing a tall, highball glass in front of Keya before sitting down next to her.

Keya was grateful, as her head was starting to hurt. Was it from all the information she'd been going through this morning?

"And they said the food will take ten minutes," Warren added. He carried a wooden chair over from another table, placed it at the end of the picnic bench, and sat down.

They chatted happily in the warm sunshine. The day felt fresh after the overnight rain and the flowers were bright and cheerful.

"What are you all doing this weekend?" Stan asked.

"Working at the cafe," Keya slurred. She stopped, and noticed Sujin glance at her with concern. She focused on the glass in front of her. Or was it two glasses?

"Millie and I are embarking on the second section of the Cotswold Way, from Wotton-under-Edge to Leckhampton Hill."

"How far is that?" asked Stan.

"Just over thirty-five miles."

"Rather you than me, and it's due to get hot this weekend." Stan lifted his glass to his lips.

"There should be some great views. Particularly in the final section as we climb up to the top of Leckhampton Hill."

"Bonkers," Stan muttered, and sipped his ale.

The food arrived, and Keya enjoyed the first part of her hummus and pickled vegetable sandwich in a homemade brown bread roll. But she struggled to swallow the final part, and her stomach felt sore.

Ten minutes later, Sujin yawned and said, "I better get back." I need to check the results of a test I'm running.

"I suppose we should all head back," Stan said in a wistful tone.

Keya didn't feel like working this afternoon. She just felt like staying in the garden and sleeping. She felt her eyelids drooping.

"Keya?" Ryan asked, getting concerned.

"Just leave me here," she mumbled.

She felt a hand shake her shoulder, and another voice urged, "Keya!"

CHAPTER TWENTY-NINE

Keya was only partly aware of someone helping her to stand up. Or was it two sets of arms urging her forward?

And there was shouting. Had something happened? She couldn't focus properly, and her arms were stiff and sore.

"Wait here!" someone called.

Were they speaking to her?

She leaned against someone. Sujin, she thought from the rich, earthy, slightly exotic smell.

"You'll be OK. Just stay with me," he urged gently.

She heard a squeal of brakes, and then she was bundled into the back of a car. A patrol car. Had she done something wrong? Had she been arrested?

Sirens blared, and she was thrown back in her seat as the car accelerated.

"It's not far. Just stay with me," Sujin urged.

And it wasn't far. The car braked sharply to a stop and hands helped her out. Why couldn't she move her arms?

She was half-carried, and half-stumbled through brown-framed entrance doors. It felt like the police station, but weren't its doors blue?

Inside, it definitely didn't smell like the police station. There was the sharp smell of bleach and an underlying … sickness. Was she in a hospital?

"What's happened?" asked an urgent, authoritative voice.

"She collapsed over lunch. I can't see any obvious cause, but …" Sujin continued speaking as Keya screwed up her eyes and tried to see where she was. Ghostly shapes of blue and pink. Why wouldn't her eyes focus, and why were her legs hurting?

She felt herself slipping until firm arms grabbed her.

"Get a wheelchair," the authoritative voice called.

"Keya, can you hear me?" the voice asked as a light hurt her eyes.

She tried to speak, but her voice was weak. "Yes," she gasped.

"I'm Doctor Lyle and I'm here to help you. Where does it hurt?"

"My head, tummy. Can't move my arms. Sore legs," she answered in a confused tone.

"Come this way," Dr Lyle instructed, and Keya felt herself being pushed along a corridor. She stopped and heard a curtain being pulled.

"I'll just be outside. Call if you need anything," Sujin said. She thought he might have touched her, but she didn't feel anything.

"Here we go," another voice said, and strong arms lifted her out of the wheelchair and onto a bed.

For the next five minutes, she was prodded and poked. Her pulse was taken, and someone listened to her heart.

She saw the doctor hold up a needle and syringe, but she wasn't sure if he had injected her until he said, "That was an antitoxin to prevent further damage to your nerves."

Nerve damage. Is that why she couldn't feel her arms and her legs were sore? Was she paralysed?

She tried to sit up. She couldn't, and her heart started to quicken.

"It's OK," the doctor reassured her with a confident tone. "The paralysis shouldn't be permanent, although it may take time for your arms to fully function again."

Shouldn't?

"Keya?" called the doctor.

Keya was aware of the curtain being pulled back and Sujin appeared, a concerned look on his face.

"She needs to calm down, otherwise the antitoxin won't work," the doctor instructed.

Sujin bent down so his face was close to Keya's. He said, "Did you hear that? You need to keep calm for the drugs to work. Panicking will only make it worse. Don't try to move for the moment. Just relax onto your pillow."

His voice was soothing, and this time Keya felt his reassuring touch as he eased her into a more comfortable position on the hospital bed.

She looked up at him and said weakly, "Thank you."

She must have drifted off to sleep because when she woke, she was outside, and the sun was on her face.

Beside her, Sujin said, "They're transferring you to Cheltenham Hospital, but don't worry, I'll stay with you."

Suddenly she was moving, rolling forward to the sound of metallic wheels. She lurched to one side and then the stretcher righted itself and rolled on again. Next, there was a sensation of being lifted and the sun was blotted out as she was wheeled into a vehicle. She must be in an ambulance.

"How are you feeling?" asked Sujin as he sat down beside her. Was he touching her hand? She couldn't feel it.

"Numb," she replied hoarsely.

"The doctor said you've stabilised and the fact you can breathe on your own is positive."

It certainly was, thought Keya. If she stopped breathing, she'd be dead.

Sujin continued, "They've given you some antibiotics so your body can fight whatever has affected you."

"What's the matter?" she managed to mutter. Adding 'with me' was too much to say.

"The doctor thinks food poisoning and I concur. They've taken a sample of blood to run tests, so hopefully we'll know soon after you arrive at Cheltenham Hospital. Why don't you try to rest?"

The ambulance wasn't using its siren, which, she thought, as it swayed, was a good thing. And she did feel tired ...

When she next woke up, she was aware of multiple noises and, in particular, the sound of an ambulance siren getting closer. Not hers. Some other poor person who was in trouble.

"Thank you. I'll take her from here. Are those her notes?" asked an efficient sounding man with an accent she couldn't place.

"I'm with her," said Sujin.

"Family?" asked the man uncertainly.

"Partner."

Despite the numbness and the pain seeping into her limbs, Keya felt a flutter in her chest. She liked the idea of Sujin calling her his partner. Although, she reminded herself, in work terms, technically they were partners, and members of the same team.

But she tried to hold on to the warm feeling of hope as bright lights, the smell of disinfectant, and multiple voices invaded her senses.

She'd been lifted from one trolley to another and the new one wheeled smoothly along corridors until they entered a ward. A woman in a bed looked at her with concern as she rolled past. A woman who looked like Peggy, her neighbour.

But then a blue curtain was pulled around her and she, Sujin, and the ebony-skinned man with the efficient voice and manner were on their own.

"This is where I leave you," said the man. "A nurse will be in to see you soon. Good luck."

"Thank you," she tried to mutter. She wasn't sure if she'd been successful, but he smiled at her sympathetically before he left.

It was just her and Sujin.

"Water," she croaked.

"I'm not sure I can give you any at the moment. We'll have to wait to see what the doctor or nurse says." Sujin looked down at her and brushed a strand of hair away from her face. At least she could feel that. And her toes were tingling. Was that a good or a bad sign?

The blue curtain was swept aside and a man and a woman wearing navy blue entered.

The dark featured man in his fifties stopped and said, "Sujin Kerr. I heard you speak about the importance of protecting forensic evidence on patients suspected of being victims of crime."

Keya thought Sujin was blushing. And she had no idea he lectured on his work. How many other attributes did Sujin have that she wasn't aware of?

"This is my partner, Sergeant Keya Varma, and she isn't a victim of crime. Or not that I'm aware of," he added thoughtfully.

"Sergeant Varma. We're still waiting for the blood test results from Cirencester, but in the meantime, do you mind if I examine you?"

Keya shook her head and prepared herself to be prodded and probed once again. She neither knew nor cared if Sujin remained in the examination area with her, but she did wonder what had happened to her uniform. She instinctively knew she wasn't wearing it.

"Your vital signs are fine, and your body is stable," the doctor said reassuringly. "Can you feel this?"

Feel what? Keya wondered.

"I think her throat is dry. Can she have some water?" Sujin asked.

"Yes, of course. Nurse Roberts?"

But the blue-clad lady had already left. She returned with a plastic glass, which she handed to Sujin. After helping Keya into a sitting position, she took the glass back and held it to Keya's lips.

Keya felt better for the water and to be sitting up. She looked at her right arm and tried to raise it. Relieved, she watched it rise from the bed but then it stopped, hovering in mid-air, refusing to move up any further. Frustrated, she allowed it to drop back on the bed.

The doctor watched as she tried the same with her left arm. But it wouldn't move. Only her fingers trembled.

"Not bad. There is movement," said the doctor.

How could he stand there and say that? Her arms weren't working. Was she paralysed?

"Try to lift your right leg."

Keya lifted her bare leg easily off the bed.

"Excellent, and the left," instructed the doctor.

Again, she lifted the leg easily, although she felt it tingle.

"It tingles," she croaked.

"That's good. You can feel it," the doctor insisted as the nurse raised the glass to Keya's lips again.

"What's wrong?" she asked.

"I'd say poison. Would you concur, Sujin?"

Sujin nodded. "Yes, I agree. Keya's been poisoned."

CHAPTER THIRTY

Poisoned! How could she have been? Who'd want to poison her? Her thoughts raced through her mind.

"Steady," the nurse reassured her, placing her hand on the top of Keya's arm. The relief of being able to feel it did calm Keya down.

"In order for the drugs to work, and to start reversing the nerve damage and paralysis, you must remain calm," the doctor told her firmly but compassionately.

"Doctor," said another blue-clad nurse as she handed him a tablet.

The doctor took the black-backed tablet and stared at it. "Of course, but rare," the doctor murmured to himself.

The nurse moved away from Keya's bed and took the tablet as the doctor stepped forward.

Sujin also moved closer, placing a protective arm on Keya's shoulder.

"Botulism," the doctor announced.

"Of course," Sujin agreed.

"Caused by a toxin produced by the bacteria Clostridium botulinum," continued the doctor. "Which attacks the central nervous system, hence your paralysis."

"How?" Keya asked. Nobody had injected her with anything, apart from the doctors, and surely nothing had been added to her food or drink.

"Easily. It's tasteless and odourless so you wouldn't even realise you were consuming it. Although rare in store-bought foods, it's surprising how easily it can develop at home. Potatoes baked in tin foil, improperly canned or preserved foods, homemade dips or sauces, or even food just left warm or unrefrigerated for too long. Especially when the temperature is high in the summer months."

"My pickled vegetable roll at lunch," she considered.

The doctor shook his head.

"Too quick. Botulism needs a minimum of four hours. Usually, it takes between eighteen and thirty-six hours, but it can take up to eight days for the symptoms to show."

What had she eaten at the cafe? Were they serving something potentially fatal? But she'd only drunk tea yesterday.

"Tea?" she asked.

"The drink or the meal?" enquired the doctor. "The drink won't be the cause. In fact, I encourage you to drink more of it, particularly herbal without milk as the antioxidants will help the paralysis and inflammation. The meal could if it contained any chutneys, tinned vegetables, or something similar which hasn't been made properly."

"Piccalilli," gasped Keya.

"What?" asked Sujin, staring down at her, his brow furrowed.

"Maitri and I tried some homemade piccalilli for the deli yesterday." Keya stopped. Maitri!

She tried but failed to grab Sujin's arm. "You must call Maitri. She might be ill."

"If you know someone else who might also have eaten the affected food, they must be checked out at their local hospital," insisted the doctor.

Sujin's eyes were wide with concern as he said, "I don't have her number."

Keya had no idea where her phone was.

"Call the cafe, or Millie, or Gilly."

"OK, keep calm. I'll do that now," and Sujin left the examination area.

Keya sat back. Her brain was racing, but her body felt tired.

"We'll keep you here in the critical care department overnight, and if you continue to respond to treatment, we'll move you onto one of the main wards tomorrow. For now, I'll leave you in the care of Nurse Roberts, but I'll be back to check on you later."

The doctor left the examination area and the round-faced nurse checked Keya's pulse and temperature.

"How long will I be in for?" Keya asked.

"Don't worry about that. Get some rest and concentrate on getting better. The quicker you do that, the sooner you'll be out of here."

The nurse smiled at Keya and helped her lie down on the bed. As she pulled the blue curtain back, a voice from the next bed cried, "Keya!"

Keya froze. "Peggy?"

"Yes, luv. I had a scare with my heart, and they rushed me here in an ambulance. Caused quite a scene in the village. All our neighbours came out to see me off. And Derek was in a flap."

"Are you OK?" Keya knew Peggy had been receiving ongoing treatment for a heart condition.

"They ran some more tests and, like you, they're keeping me here overnight for observation. But what's wrong with you? Did I hear food poisoning?"

"Not at the cafe," Keya replied hastily. "It might be from some homemade piccalilli I tasted last night."

"Yes, you have to be careful with that," Peggy conceded. "But how are you feeling now?"

"Tired, numb, and tingly. I can't move my left arm, but my right arm is feeling better." She lifted it again to make sure. "And so are my legs." She wriggled her toes.

"The rest will do you good," Peggy reasoned. "You're always rushing around."

In the silence which followed, Keya realised how ill some of the patients she could see were, hooked up to beeping machines and monitors.

She felt better, but also concerned that the doctors classified her illness as critical as the others in the ward. But at least she had Peggy's cheerful demeanour to keep up her spirits.

"And who's this?" asked Peggy as Sujin reached Keya's bed. "Haven't I seen you before?"

"Hi, I'm Sujin. A colleague of Keya's," Sujin introduced himself.

"You don't look like a policeman."

"I'm not. My title is crime scene technician."

"Which means what?"

"I examine crime scenes, collect evidence, and work on the forensic side of an investigation." Sujin removed his glasses and ran his hand through his dark hair.

"Hey, you're that fiddle player. I knew I'd seen you before."

"I'm with the Celtic Twisters."

"You played at our local pub, The Dog and Duck," Peggy remembered.

"That's right. And Keya and Ryan were there."

"Yes. They were."

Nurse Roberts approached. "Now that's quite enough of that. Other patients are resting and so should you two. I'm going to have to ask you to leave," she said to Sujin.

"Maitri!" Keya cried.

"I'll just be a minute," Sujin promised.

"You have five. And then you need to leave Keya to sleep." The nurse turned and strode away.

Sujin leaned over Keya and said, "I got hold of the cafe - they're all worried, by the way, and hope you feel better soon. Gilly wanted to come over, but I told her I wasn't sure about visiting hours in the critical care unit. That only made her worse. But, eventually, I spoke to your sister, and she's fine. She can't understand why you are ill as you both tasted the same things, and she has no side effects."

"It takes time," Keya warned.

"I know. Which is why I told Maitri to go to Cirencester Hospital to get checked out. She protested. So I asked Gilly to take her, and she seemed delighted to have something to do."

"Thank you," said Keya, suddenly feeling weary again. She closed her eyes.

CHAPTER THIRTY-ONE

Keya woke the next morning feeling groggy and stiff. She wriggled her toes and gently raised both legs to check they still worked. They did, and she didn't feel any tingling, which she thought was a good sign.

Next, she tried her right arm. She was able to move it out of the white sheets which covered her. It took a lot of effort, and it was slow going, but finally she placed it on top of the sheets and lay back with relief.

Turning her head and her thoughts to her left arm, she concentrated really hard. Nothing. Her arm wouldn't move. Feeling her heart start to beat faster and the panic set in, she took a deep breath, held it, and breathed out. Everyone had told her panicking would only make things worse, and she knew they were right.

She lay back listening to the rhythmic sigh of machines and the beeping of others.

"You awake, Keya?" called Peggy.

"Yes," Keya replied.

Putting her right arm to use, she managed to shuffle her body into a half lying, half sitting position. It wasn't great, but at least she could see Peggy and the rest of the ward.

Peggy smiled and acknowledged, "You slept a lot. Do you feel better?"

"I do," Keya admitted. "And you?"

"I like my own bed. And there's too much noise in here. Hopefully, they'll let me out after the doctor has checked me over this morning. Just a false alarm, I'm sure."

Keya hoped her neighbour was right, although she had her reservations. Why would they have kept Peggy in overnight in the critical care unit if they weren't concerned about her? Or me for that matter, Keya thought.

A light-blue clad orderly appeared at the entrance to the ward, pushing a trolley holding several tall stainless-steel flasks.

"Oh good. Time for a cup of tea," Peggy said, and she reached down to a cable dangling below her bed and pressed a button.

A different navy blue-clad nurse from the previous day pushed past the drinks trolley and approached Peggy's bed. "Good morning," she said curtly.

Peggy ignored her tone and said, "Can you help me and my friend to sit up, so we can enjoy our morning cuppa?"

"Of course," and the nurse helped Peggy sit up, rearranging her pillows behind her back.

Peggy smiled at Keya. Did Peggy really need so much help?

When the nurse approached Keya, she observed, "You've managed to move yourself a bit. What movement do you have in your arms?"

"None in my left still, but my right is working better."

"Good. The doctor will visit after breakfast."

Keya was grateful for her tea, even though she felt like a small child as the orderly held the grey plastic cup up to her lips so she could sip from it.

"Better than home, this is," said Peggy cheerfully. "And we get to enjoy breakfast in bed, too."

Breakfast was a choice of cornflakes, Weetabix, or bran flakes. Keya chose bran flakes, which were served in a grey plastic bowl, a strawberry yogurt, and a slice of brown toast with orange marmalade.

It wasn't gourmet, but it was simple, and Keya found she was hungry, since she hadn't eaten the night before.

A young orderly in a light-blue uniform arrived at Keya's bedside and said, "I've come to help. Would you like me to feed you?"

No, Keya thought instinctively. But what if she couldn't feed herself? She looked down at the table, which had been swung across her bed. Its supporting stand and wheels were to her right.

"Can you raise the table?" she asked.

"Of course."

But even with the table raised, Keya couldn't spoon cereal on her own and raise it to her mouth. In the end, she allowed her cheerful helper to collect a spoonful of bran flakes and lift it to her lips, where she was able to spoon it into her own mouth.

It was laborious and Keya felt self-conscious, but whenever she looked across at Peggy, her neighbour smiled and nodded her encouragement.

The assistant also helped her eat her yogurt, but at least she could grip her toast herself and lift it to her mouth. Eating was not going to be fun until her right arm was working properly, and by the end of the meal, she felt exhausted.

"Thank you," she said to her cheerful helper, who wheeled the table out of the way.

"No problem. And I'm on duty all day, so if you need any help with headphones or the like, just call?"

"How?" Keya asked.

The orderly reached under her bed and scooped up a cable like the one next to Peggy's bed. Attached to it there was a flat red button. "With this. Do you want to practise pressing it?"

Feeling rather ridiculous at having to practise anything so simple, but realising the orderly wouldn't leave until she did, Keya pressed the button.

"Excellent," the orderly praised her as if Keya had reached an important goal. Perhaps she had.

The nurse appeared at the entrance to the ward and the orderly left Keya, and said as she approached the nurse, "I was just checking Keya could use the call button. What would you like me to do now?"

The two blue-clad figures left the ward.

A few minutes later, the senior nurse reappeared with the doctor who'd seen Keya the previous day. They approached the first bed and drew the curtain around it.

"Derek should be here after the doctor's rounds," Peggy said. "What about you? Is that attentive young man coming back to see you?"

"I don't know," Keya admitted. It was a Saturday, so she wasn't sure who'd come to see her. People had plans. Millie and Ryan were running the Cotswold Way. Millie. The Cafe. She was supposed to be covering.

She should call someone, but she couldn't. She didn't have her phone.

"Are you OK?" asked Peggy.

"I'm supposed to be at the cafe this morning and I can't call anyone to sort it out."

"Don't worry about that. They'll know you're in hospital, and I'm sure they can manage without you."

Keya sank back into her pillows. In truth, they could manage without her.

"Why the glum look?" asked the doctor as he approached Keya's bed.

The nurse pulled the blue curtain screen around them.

"I was just thinking that while I'm stuck in here, work will carry on without me."

"That's a good thing, isn't it? Give you time to rest and recuperate. And how are you feeling this morning?"

"Better, thank you," Keya replied politely.

The doctor went through his checks and then asked her to raise her limbs. Her right arm was improving each time, but her left one remained limply by her side.

"We'll start you with physiotherapy treatment straight away, to help your movement. Otherwise you've reacted well to treatment and I'm confident that there'll be no long-term damage." He glanced across at her left arm.

Not that confident, Keya thought.

"Which means we'll also move you to the Knightsbridge Ward for your ongoing care with us. I'm sure they'll look after you very well there."

"How long will I be in?" asked Keya.

"Two or three days, I suspect, or until they're sure there are no after additional effects from your poisoning."

Keya didn't want to know what additional affects the doctor was talking about.

And two or three days.

What about Daisy's case?

CHAPTER THIRTY-TWO

Soon after the doctor left, an orderly appeared and said to Keya, "I'm here to take you to the Knightsbridge Ward."

"That sounds posh," Peggy remarked.

"What about you?" Keya asked her.

"They won't let me out just yet. Said they need to keep an eye on me, so I'll also be moving wards. But I should be out of here soon. I look forward to enjoying a cup of tea with you back home. We might even persuade Derek to make it for us."

Peggy smiled as Keya was wheeled away on her bed.

Keya's new ward had a less clinical and more relaxed feel about it. The staff wore a range of coloured uniforms from the navy and light blue she'd seen in the critical care ward, to white, pale green, and even royal blue.

They all smiled at her as she was wheeled into a ward with six beds, of which four were occupied. She was parked in an empty space at the far end.

"Welcome, Keya," said a nurse as the orderly left. "Are you happy lying down, or would you like to sit up?"

"Sit up," said Keya. She wasn't spending all day sleeping. What she really wanted was a book to read or her phone and EarPods, but she didn't have anything. And there was nobody to ask to get them for her.

"Tea or coffee?" asked an elderly orderly.

"Tea, please," Keya replied, realising that it wasn't all bad. There was nobody in the bed next to her and the other patients looked frail and elderly. She already missed Peggy.

"There you are," cried Sujin. He strode into the ward carrying a small overnight bag. Her overnight bag. Ryan and Stan followed him, and Keya thought she could hear Inspector Evans' baritone Welsh voice.

"They wouldn't let us see you in the critical care ward and then they said you'd moved, but it took them half an hour to tell us where to. How are you?" Sujin asked, his face full of concern as he stood beside her bed.

Ryan and Stan moved to the far side, beside the window.

"Better. Look, I can lift my right arm." This time, Keya was able to move it up to her chin. She didn't mention her left arm, and neither did Sujin, even though he glanced at it.

"Where shall I put your tea, luv?" asked the elderly orderly.

"Um, I can't drink by myself," Keya admitted.

"I can help with that," Stan volunteered. "I had to help my missus last year when she fell and broke her arm."

As Stan took the cup from the orderly, Keya noticed the dark circles around Sujin's eyes. "Late night with the band?" she asked.

"Band?" Stan repeated, holding the grey plastic cup to Keya's mouth. "He slept at the station last night."

Keya sipped the over-stewed tea before narrowing her eyes. She was sure Sujin was wearing a different set of clothes from the previous day.

Perhaps Sujin noticed her questioning look as he said, "Like you and Ryan, I now keep a spare set of clothes at the station."

"Is there a break in Daisy's case?" Keya asked.

"No, we're at a dead end with that," Ryan admitted.

"So why were you pulling an all-nighter?" Keya asked Sujin in confusion.

"To try to find out what poisoned you. And it wasn't the piccalilli, or your sandwich from the pub," Sujin replied.

"How do you know?" Keya enquired.

"I ran tests. Maitri gave me both jars of piccalilli you sampled. She's OK, by the way, and was somewhat disgruntled about going to hospital until she realised how serious your condition was. They weren't very happy in The Twelve Bells pub when I asked for samples of the hummus and pickled vegetables, but they were horrified that they might have caused you to collapse. But it wasn't anything to do with them either."

"So what was it?"

"That's what we'd all like to know," Sujin replied, regarding her with a sympathetic look.

"Sergeant," Inspector Evans declared as he approached the group around her bed. "I've just spoken to the medical staff and you're not out of the woods yet. They're keeping you in to make sure none of your internal organs are affected."

"Oh," Keya replied, not sure how to take such cheery news.

"So use the time to rest," added the inspector.

"I can't sleep all day," Keya protested. "And I can't read a book. And I haven't got my phone or EarPods to listen to music or a story, so it's going to be a bit dull."

"I've got your phone," Sujin said. "Gilly and Maitri collected it from Cirencester Hospital, along with your uniform."

He placed it on the bed and, with some effort, Keya manoeuvred her arm around until she could press the button with her index finger. The screen came to life and on it she saw alerts for messages and missed calls.

She'd deal with those later.

"And Maitri also collected some clothes. Perhaps she also picked up your EarPods." Sujin gave her another sympathetic look and said, "Your family are coming in this afternoon, so I'll ask Maitri to bring some headphones, and perhaps a tablet so you can watch a film or TV."

"But what we need to do is find out how you were poisoned, and if it was a deliberate attack," Inspector Evans stated.

Keya's eyes opened wide. Was she the subject of a police investigation?

For clarity, she asked, "Are you opening a case on me?"

"We are, Sergeant," confirmed Inspector Evans. "And we've all agreed to work over the weekend to try to solve it."

"But there's no need for that. What about your plans? Ryan, you and Millie were running the next section of the Cotswold Way."

"That can wait, and anyway, Millie's working at the cafe."

Keya felt her cheeks colour guiltily.

"It's OK," Ryan added. "We'd much rather help you."

"So," continued Inspector Evans, "apart from your lunchtime sandwich, and the piccalilli, what else have you consumed in the last week?"

"Week?" Keya exclaimed.

"Yes, botulism can take several days to have an effect," Sujin explained.

Keya thought back. "I had fruit and yoghurt and a slice of toast for breakfast on Friday. On Thursday, I had a baked potato with salads and coleslaw left over from the cafe. At lunchtime I made an omelette for Theo Watson and myself, and breakfast was similar to Friday."

"Lunchtime on Thursday would put it in the critical time period. What did you have?" Sujin asked.

"Only an omelette, and so did Theo. Should we check how he is?"

"All in good time, Sergeant," confirmed Inspector Evans.

"Any pickled vegetables with the omelette, or chutneys or sauces?"

"Oh, I did have some of Daisy's mum's hot sauce."

Inspector Evans and Sujin exchanged a glance.

"What?" asked Keya.

"Did Theo have any of it?" asked Sujin.

"No, he said he didn't feel like it."

"And can you remember what you ate on Wednesday?"

Keya listed her meals for Wednesday and Tuesday and answered Sujin's and the Inspector's follow-up questions.

When they'd finished, she felt weary and drained, and still at a loss as to how she fell ill.

"I think that's enough for now," said the nurse as she approached the bed. "The other patients need their rest, and so does Keya."

"Of course," Inspector Evans acknowledged. "And thank you for allowing us to speak to Sergeant Varma."

Stan and Ryan said their goodbyes and followed Inspector Evans out of the ward.

Sujin hung back.

"You're definitely looking better," he said. "I'll come back later, probably tonight."

"What about the band?"

"Don't worry. Jerry can stand in for me." Sujin bent down and kissed her forehead.

As he stood up, they both blushed.

Sujin smiled shyly and said, "See you later."

CHAPTER THIRTY-THREE

Keya felt tired after her team had left and she dozed for a while until an earnest young woman with a blonde ponytail and a white uniform arrived beside her bed.

"Hi, I'm Laura. Your physiotherapist. Do you have anything else to wear?"

"There should be something in the bag beside my bed," Keya replied, wondering what Maitri had packed for her.

Laura pulled the blue curtain round for privacy and placed Keya's overnight bag on the bed. Opening it, she removed Keya's EarPods, and some magazines Maitri must have bought. Keya was grateful, as she could probably flick through and read them more easily than she could a book.

"Here we are. A pair of tracksuit bottoms and a T-shirt."

Keya rarely wore her tracksuit bottoms, and she wondered why Maitri had chosen them, but she was pleased she had. The elastic waist would be much easier to pull up and didn't need fastening like trousers with a zip.

Laura helped Keya dress, assessing her range of movement, until she was standing beside her bed, fully clothed. She had been apprehensive about swinging her legs to the edge of her bed and then using her right arm to push herself upright. And she was relieved her legs held her weight.

Laura pulled the curtain back and encouraged Keya to walk the length of the ward and back. The other patients lying in their beds either slept or watched her with vacant or bored expressions.

Keya couldn't remember when she'd felt so much joy for doing such a simple thing as walking. She marched across the ward again and out to the nurses' station, her right arm swinging. But her left arm still hung limply by her side.

When she returned to her bed, Laura smiled and asked, "Did that feel good?"

"Yes," Keya replied, grinning.

Laura then stood in front of Keya and instructed, "Lift your right arm and rest it on my shoulder."

Keya did as she was told.

"Good. Put it down and lift your left arm."

Keya thought she felt her arm twitch, but it didn't move.

"OK. Not to worry. But we'll need to do some work with that arm."

Laura spent another five minutes instructing Keya to perform mobility and strength exercises, including squats, and Keya was actually relieved to climb back onto her bed. Laura massaged her left arm and promised to come and see her again in the afternoon.

The activity had energised Keya, and she considered what to do next. Her phone was lying on the portable table, along with the magazines Maitri had packed for her. She pressed her call button, and a nurse appeared.

"Please, can you move my table across so I can reach the things on it?"

"Of course, dear."

"And is it possible to have a cup of tea?"

"I can fetch you a glass of water. Tea will be served with lunch in half an hour."

Satisfied with her set up, Keya checked the missed calls and messages on her phone. She had three voice messages from her increasingly panicky sounding mother. On the last one, Keya's sister Zivah must have taken the phone as she said calmly that she hoped

Keya was feeling better and they'd visit as soon as they were allowed to.

There were other messages from friends and family and a funny cartoon meme from the Wimsey family wishing her well.

Lunch was a vegetarian pie with lumpy mashed potatoes and over-boiled vegetables, followed by fruit crumble and custard. It wasn't very appetising, and she picked one-handedly at what she could before giving up on the soggy pastry of the pie and moving on to her pudding. But it was cold, and the custard had congealed.

She was grateful when the orderly reappeared and served her a cup of tea with a couple of plain biscuits. She was just settling down to read a woman's health magazine when her mother swept into the ward, followed by her elderly father and Zivah.

Keya looked past them, and Zivah said, "I left Kaami at home with his dad. I wasn't sure about bringing him to a hospital."

Keya was disappointed not to see her young nephew, but as she looked at Zivah, she thought her sister needed the bed more than she did. Zivah's face was haggard, and her eyes were dull.

"Kaami still not sleeping?" asked Keya.

"It's more than that. He keeps throwing up his milk and then bawling his head off. I don't know what to do." Zivah ran her hand through her long black hair.

"I've told you, massage his tummy with the mixture I've given you," said their mother, who they all called Amma.

"I do massage his stomach, and wind him, but he still cries. The health visitor just sympathises and tells me he'll grow out of it. But he can't grow if he doesn't keep his milk down." Zivah looked close to tears.

"I'm sorry, sis. And I'm not much help stuck in here."

"I've told you, come and stay with us and I can help you," Amma urged.

Their father, who they affectionately called Appa, looked horrified by the idea.

"No. I need to stay with Aadi. And he's a good father and helps when he can. Like looking after Kaami while I'm here visiting Keya." Zivah leaned closer and asked, "How are you?"

"I'm fine. Relieved. It was all rather a blur yesterday, but losing the use of my arms, and thinking my legs might also be paralysed was scary."

"Are they OK now?" enquired Zivah, a shocked expression on her face.

"My legs are fine. Sore from the physio making me do squats this morning." Keya grinned before continuing, "And I have more movement in my right arm. It's only my left which is still refusing to work, but the physio is hopeful the paralysis won't be permanent."

Amma gasped. Then she turned to Appa and said, "We must find Keya a good Indian doctor."

"There are good doctors here, and some of them are even Indian," replied Appa levelly. "I'm sure they're doing their best for Keya."

"They are," agreed Keya.

"These things take time," added Appa wisely.

Amma bowed her head in acceptance.

"So you'll be needing someone to help out at the cafe until you're back on your feet," Zivah said, brightly.

"I'm not sure. Millie is doing a great job …" Keya regarded her sister. She could see that Zivah wanted to come back to work. "But I'm sure she'd welcome your help. Especially now the weather is better, and then there's the school holidays, which will attract more customers."

"But what about Kaami?" Amma demanded.

"He can go to nursery."

"Nursery! Let me look after him."

Zivah glanced at Appa, who inclined his head in agreement. "Well, if you're sure he won't be too much trouble."

"Trouble. You've no idea what you girls were like. And Maitri!" exclaimed their mother.

Keya settled back on her pillows as they all listened to Amma recalling stories from their childhood.

Keya wasn't sure her mother would ever leave, but Laura returned and said, "I hope you don't mind, but I need to do some work with Keya to make sure she's fighting fit as soon as possible."

"Of course. And I'm glad you're doing so well, Keya. You gave us quite a scare," Amma said.

Appa gave her a look full of warmth and love and Zivah squeezed her arm before leaving and said, "Maitri will visit later. She couldn't get away this afternoon as the deli, and her ice cream stall in particular, are busy today."

Keya completed her work with Laura and then, feeling weary, she slept until tea was served. She looked down at her plate of egg sandwiches in limp white bread, wondering how they would sustain her until the morning, but as she bit into one, she discovered it was an improvement on lunch.

Maitri appeared as her plate was being cleared away, and she gave her a huge hug.

"I was so worried about you. And I thought it was my fault for making you try those chutneys and piccalilli, but Sujin assures me they aren't to blame. But what is, do you think?"

"I don't know. I just hope it isn't anything from the cafe."

Maitri's eyes widened. "Or we could be closed down."

"Don't say that. I'm sure it's nothing to do with our food." Keya crossed the fingers of her right hand, hoping she was right.

Maitri reached into her bag and removed a tablet, a packet of biscuits, and several varieties of crisps together with some chocolate brownies.

"These should keep you going."

"Thanks. They're a great improvement on the food in here. But you better hide them in my cupboard in case they're not allowed."

As Maitri hid the goodies she'd brought, Keya added, "And that's not my tablet."

"No, it's mine and I've uploaded some programmes for you to watch. If you can connect to the Wi-Fi in here, then you'll be able to watch others too."

"Thank you. And for the magazines. That was a brilliant idea, as I can't hold a book."

Maitri smiled and admitted, "It was Gilly's idea. She was desperate to visit earlier, but Aunt Beanie told her to wait and let you have time with Amma and Appa. But she said she'll come tomorrow."

Maitri paused before enquiring, "How long do you think they'll keep you in?"

"I'm not sure. They said they wanted to make sure there aren't any additional complications."

Maitri regarded her sympathetically and said, "I suppose you're in the right place. Even if the food isn't great."

CHAPTER THIRTY-FOUR

Keya and Maitri continued to chat until Sujin arrived carrying a brown paper bag with the aroma of coconut, cardamom, and other Indian spices.

"I've heard the food isn't great in here, so I brought you a very mild coconut curry. The nurse said it would be OK, but you can't eat it in the ward."

"Time to get up," Keya said cheerfully.

"And I should head home. Amma and Appa will want an update." Maitri gave Keya a quick hug before she left.

Sujin moved the portable table out of the way and pulled back the sheets, so Keya could swing her legs out of the bed and stand up. He led her to a breakout area along the corridor which looked out over the car park and beyond it the lido, Cheltenham's open air swimming pool.

Sujin had also brought food for himself, so Keya didn't feel guilty as she tucked into her tasty curry. This would keep her going until the morning.

"Any news?" Keya asked between mouthfuls.

"I visited Theo Watson, and he was appalled to hear you were ill. I took samples of all the food you used to make the omelettes and the hot sauce. I hope you don't mind, but I went to your house with Maitri and removed samples from your fridge to test, including the leftover coleslaw."

"Oh, I hope it's not that," Keya protested.

"So do I. But we'll have to wait until tomorrow for all the results."

They finished their meal and Keya sat back, full and satisfied. "That was lovely, thank you."

Sujin looked at her before asking, "What are you going to do when you're discharged?"

"Finish the Daisy Bentham case. And the cafe and deli are getting busier, and there's Gilly's party at the end of the month, and then the open-air cinema."

Sujin held up both hands. "Whoa. Slow down. I meant, how are you going to recover and recuperate?"

"Recuperate?" Keya asked in a bemused voice. "I'll be fine. I just need to know what happened to Daisy."

"And then there'll be another Daisy, or Duncan, or Donna. What about giving yourself a break? Even if you don't like to admit it, your body suffered a severe bout of poisoning, and it does need to rest and recover. And you can't maintain the pace you've been running around at."

Keya wasn't sure how to reply. This was yet another side to Sujin she hadn't seen before. A firm, sensible, but perceptive and persuasive side.

"You're right," she muttered. "But there's always so much to do. And it's my responsibility to look after the Cotswolds. That's my role. And then there's the cafe. I rely on other people too much as it is."

"Then perhaps you need to re-think your priorities."

"You sound like my mum."

Keya stared out of the window. She enjoyed being busy, and she didn't want to give up her cafe. But she knew she wasn't involved with it in the hands-on way she'd thought she would be.

Her rural engagement role was interesting, and she enjoyed meeting farmers, visiting schools, and helping at community functions, but she knew she'd never stop rural crime. Nobody could without more resources and more people in the role other than just her.

Perhaps she should concentrate on that and forget about the major crimes Inspector Evan's team dealt with, but they were the ones that gave her the most satisfaction.

"Keya?" Sujin prompted.

"I was just thinking through what you said. I know I do a lot, but I'm not sure what I should give up, if anything."

"You don't need to make any long-term decisions now," Sujin reasoned. "Although I think, while you have the time and space, you should consider what you want your life to look like over the next few years." He regarded her kindly, and she wasn't sure if she saw something else in his expression. Hope perhaps?

"But it's your recovery after you leave hospital I'm concerned about for now. I really don't think you should charge straight back into work of any kind. Since our discussion at The Swan Hotel, have you thought any more about a holiday?"

Keya shook her head.

Sujin placed his hand on her right one and murmured, "I really think you should."

CHAPTER THIRTY-FIVE

Keya's first visitors on Sunday, after she'd completed an early morning session of physiotherapy with Laura, were Dotty, Gilly, and Aunt Beanie.

"We're not really supposed to visit out of hours, but we persuaded the duty nurse to let us see you, as we've all got to get to work," Aunt Beanie greeted her.

"Which is true," Gilly agreed.

"I really wanted to come yesterday," a worried-looking Dotty said. "But Aunt Beanie said we should let your family see you."

"You're here now, and it's great to see you all and you'll brighten up what would otherwise be a dull Sunday morning."

"Can't you read?' Dotty asked.

"Only magazines. Thank you for suggesting those, Gilly."

"Oh, I'm so glad they're useful. Maitri and I weren't sure what to get, so we bought a selection."

"I'm particularly enjoying the food ones, and I've found a couple of recipes I'd like to try out for the cafe."

"But you mustn't worry about that now," Dotty insisted.

Keya looked at her and asked, "What work are you doing today?" She suspected she already knew the answer.

Dotty blushed and replied, "Aunt Beanie and I are working in the kitchen at the cafe. And Zivah's working front of house. We've persuaded Millie and Ryan to both have a day off and run the Cotswold Way."

"I'm pleased about that, but I hope you'll be OK, and Zivah …"

"We saw her briefly this morning, and she seemed relieved to be having a break. I think baby Kaami is rather demanding."

"He is," Keya confirmed.

"So your cafe is in good hands. Although we mustn't be too long. Mick's doing an early morning shift, but then he wanted to visit a garden. You wouldn't think that's his thing by looking at him," Aunt Beanie commented.

"I suppose it's being in prison for so long," Keya reflected. "He appreciates nature. I know he wants to travel when he's saved up some money. Talking of which, Dotty, everyone keeps telling me I should take a holiday. I don't want to go anywhere too exotic, but would you be interested in a short break, somewhere in the UK?"

"Oh, my course has a break at the end of June, and I'm thinking of accepting a commission to provide some antiques for a hotel in the Lake District. Do you want to join me when I go to visit the hotel?"

"What about the outdoor cinema event?" Gilly asked, in an uptight tone.

"When's that?" Dotty asked.

"The 6th July."

"That's OK. I'll probably visit next weekend to confirm the job and look round. Then I can come back and start sourcing what I need, and we can go back up after the cinema event. What do you think, Keya?"

"I'm not sure. As long as I can sort out the cafe …"

"Don't worry about that," Aunt Beanie instructed. "We'll make sure it's all covered. And you will need a break. And I don't think you should be doing too much when you're discharged from here, even for the events we already have planned." She gave Keya a knowing look and Keya presumed she meant Gilly's party. "Who knows what internal damage the poison did?"

"That's why I'm still stuck in here," Keya groaned. But actually, she was now looking forward to a relaxing Sunday reading magazines and watching the TV programmes Maitri had downloaded for her. And if lunch was as bad as the previous day, she could always graze on Maitri's snacks.

"Time to go," Aunt Beanie announced.

Dotty placed a box of chocolates on the bedside table and a cookery book. "I'm not sure if you can read this, but you might like the pictures."

"I'm not a child. Oh, I see. You mean because it's too heavy to hold up to read. Sorry, I didn't mean to snap at you," apologised Keya. "And thank you. It does look interesting. Is it one on baking?"

"Yes."

Gilly put a tin of biscuits on the table, and Aunt Beanie added some packets of fruit and nuts and some cartons of fruit juice. Keya realised she'd have to be careful she didn't put on weight, but at least these treats would be a welcome addition to the hospital food.

She said goodbye to her friends and settled down to read Dotty's cookbook.

The hot drinks trolley came, and she was enjoying one of Gilly's biscuits with a cup of tea and a recipe about coconut crunch bars when Sujin appeared.

He strode across the room to her bed, grinning. "I think I've found what poisoned you."

"Really?" she replied, offering him a biscuit. "It wasn't the cafe coleslaw, was it?"

"No, it was Daisy's mum's hot sauce."

CHAPTER THIRTY-SIX

Keya stared at Sujin. Finally, she gasped, "But I hardly had any."

"You didn't need to. The hot sauce was full of Clostridium botulinum bacteria. And as I told you, the toxin they produce is tasteless and odourless."

Keya's thoughts raced in one direction.

"Daisy."

"That was my immediate thought, too," Sujin agreed. "I've asked the lab to test for the Clostridium botulinum bacteria but, as they're being so slow at the moment, and it's a Sunday, I took the sample of Daisy's blood that I had to the lab at Cirencester Hospital, in person. I've asked them to run a test and see if the bacterium in the sample matches yours."

"And if it doesn't? And there are no bacteria?"

"It'll only have cost me a few pints of beer and a couple of tickets to one of our music evenings."

Keya looked at Sujin and noticed the circles under his eyes. Reaching out, she touched his arm and said in a gentle voice, "Thank you for helping me."

Sujin gulped. "I thought I was going to lose you before we've even got to know each other. The other evening, sitting by the stream, it was so easy to relax with you. And I can talk about my work, and the band,

and a myriad of other subjects, and you seem interested in all of them."

"Of course I'm interested. You know so much. I'm fascinated."

"Is that all? You are fascinated?"

"Intrigued, full of awe. Shall I go on?" Keya joked.

"No, and speaking of awe, I'm so impressed with how well you're coping with your poisoning, and being here in hospital."

"I'm not that good a patient, but at least I can throw my energy into my physio sessions. And look, my right arm is nearly back to normal." She raised her arm and touched his chest.

He didn't ask about her left arm, and she didn't mention it. One arm at a time.

She felt his phone vibrate.

"I better take the call out of the ward," Sujin said reluctantly.

Keya watched his retreating back.

He wasn't the tall, handsome, confident figure she'd imagined herself with. Indeed, there were times when he seemed to shrink into the background, but she'd also seen a different, energised, and at ease side of him when he played his violin, or fiddle as he termed it.

And he was compassionate, and kind, and understanding. And interesting. What else could she want in a man?

And who else would, or was, doing so much to help her in her current situation? It was clear from those dark circles under his eyes that he was worried and that he'd been working hard to establish exactly what had poisoned her.

And it was as innocuous as a couple of teaspoons of hot sauce eaten with an omelette at Mill House.

Sujin returned to the ward with a grim expression. "The Cirencester Hospital lab has confirmed that the toxin in Daisy's blood matches yours. So she died of botulism or botulinum poisoning."

"Can you tell from the blood sample if we were poisoned by the same source?"

"Scientifically, no. But surely the coincidence is too much? How many other sources of Clostridium botulinum bacteria are out there?"

Keya shuddered. She didn't like to speculate and knew she wouldn't be tasting any sauces or pickles at the deli for a while.

Then she remembered part of her conversation with Theo over

lunch. "Theo said Daisy only occasionally had the sauce. Usually he had it. So why was he not affected, and Daisy was?"

"That's something our colleagues will need to discover."

"Oh, no!"

"What?" asked Sujin.

"We could be looking at the possibility that Doreen poisoned her own daughter. She'll be devastated." At least Keya thought she would. She remembered the stricken look and the cry of grief when Doreen arrived at the standing stones early on midsummer morning.

But why had she been there so early? She said she'd heard about her daughter's death in the village, but she lived alone, outside the main part of the village. So how did she know about it, and why was she up and about so early?

"That would be terrible," Sujin agreed. "A mother accidentally poisoning her own daughter."

Sujin was still in the ward when the orderly arrived and handed out Sunday lunch. He took one look at the mush under her chrome plate cover and whisked her away to the Blue Spa Restaurant in the oldest part of the hospital.

Her creamy mushroom fettuccine with salad was a vast improvement on the food provided in the ward and she tucked in with enthusiasm.

"Why can't we get something like this on the wards?" she mumbled through a mouthful of pasta. She swallowed and continued, "Then I'd understand why we're only served a light sandwich supper."

"I'm glad you're enjoying it." Sujin smiled at her before biting into his toasted panini.

When they'd both finished, Keya felt full and tired. She said, "Thank you for that, and there's no need to bring me anything tonight. I can manage with the hospital sandwiches and all the snacks everyone has brought me. Not a single grape, though. What does that tell you?"

"That your friends and family know you well. Would you still like me to visit?"

"I would, but you need your rest as well. I think you'll have a busy start to the week."

After Sujin left, Keya settled herself onto her bed and flicked through Dotty's cookbook until Laura appeared for her afternoon physio session.

This time they left the ward and went to Laura's rehabilitation gym where Keya was subjected to more squats, and dumbbell raises with her right hand. When they returned to the ward, Inspector Evans, wearing his on-duty brown suit, and a uniformed Constable Warren Sparrow, were beside her bed. The inspector was sitting in a chair sipping from a grey plastic cup and flicking through one of her magazines.

Warren was staring out of the window when she entered, but he turned when the Inspector said, "It's a relief to see you up and about."

"Thanks. I've just been worked hard by my physio. My legs will be stronger when I leave than when I came in, and my right arm is nearly back to normal."

Again, nobody mentioned her limp left arm, which hung uselessly as she climbed onto her bed and propped herself up on her pillows.

"So, to what do I owe this visit?" she asked, flippantly.

"We need to conduct a formal interview with respect to your poisoning," replied the inspector.

"Yes, of course," Keya replied contritely.

"Tea, luv?" asked an orderly carrying a grey plastic cup and saucer.

"Yes, please." Keya took the cup and noticed the biscuits sitting on the saucer. A packet of Scottish shortbread.

"And would you like a top up, Inspector?"

"I wouldn't say no. Thank you."

Warren wasn't asked if he wanted anything.

When they were settled with their refreshments, Inspector Evans cleared his throat and began, "Tell me what happened, in your own words, on the day you visited Mill House and made lunch for yourself and Theo Watson."

Even though she'd written up a report about the visit, Keya recounted everything as best she could, including the conversation over lunch with Theo.

"So Mr Watson didn't have any of the hot sauce?"

"No, he chose the tomato chutney."

"But he did eat it on other occasions?" pressed the inspector.

"I believe so, when Daisy cooked Mexican meals." Keya gasped. "Daisy's sister, Zoe, told me she had lunch at Mill House on the Sunday before Midsummer. She said she enjoyed the meals as her father was very traditional in his eating habits."

"Constable, make a note to check the hot sauce bottle for fingerprints and to ask Theo Watson and Zoe Bentham who had the hot sauce at lunch on Sunday. And we also need to find out if there were any other guests at the lunch and, if so, if they had any of the sauce."

"So you think the hot sauce killed Daisy?" Keya asked.

"I do, although to be thorough, I'll check that Sujin has tested the other foods in the kitchen."

When Keya had finished her statement and the inspector had run out of questions, she asked, "So what now, sir?"

"We need to establish if Daisy did eat the hot sauce, and then devise a timeline to see if it's feasible that it was the cause of her death."

"Will you speak to Doreen Bentham, since she made it?"

"I'll ask Sue to do that with young Warren here. It's a tricky one, telling a mother she may have caused her daughter's death. But I don't really want to do so until we are certain of the source of Daisy's poisoning."

"You will keep me updated on the case, won't you, sir?"

"I don't think I'll need to," replied Inspector Evans. "You have your own crime scene technician to do that!"

CHAPTER THIRTY-SEVEN

Keya's mind raced with possibilities after Inspector Evans and Warren left on Sunday afternoon.

Tea was an improvement on the day before with a Greek salad supplemented by some of Aunt Beanie's fruit and nuts. She also had one of Maitri's brownies as her pudding.

Deciding there was nothing more she could do on a Sunday evening, she watched several shows Maitri had downloaded on the tablet, including a comedy set in a restaurant, which she found particularly relatable. The lights were turned off early in the ward and she decided she might as well sleep.

Monday was far more frustrating, as nobody visited, and she had no idea what was happening with Daisy's case. Or her own for that matter.

Sujin did respond to some of her messages, but she could tell he was distracted, so she thought she better leave him alone.

After another uninspiring tea of sandwiches, she was considering taking herself down to the Blue Spa Restaurant or the hospital's cafe when Sujin appeared carrying a colourful bouquet of summer flowers. The aroma immediately filled the ward.

"Thank you, they're lovely."

"Dotty suggested something seasonal and local, and we both decided lilies weren't appropriate," Sujin replied. "They also come in a vase, so we don't have to worry about finding one."

He unwrapped the flowers and placed the glass vase on top of the portable cupboard beside Keya's bed.

Keya stared at him expectantly.

"You want to know what progress we've made with the cases?"

"Of course. I've been sitting here by myself all day wondering what you're all doing and what you've found out."

"My day wasn't particularly interesting. After visiting Mill House again and collecting food samples, I spent all day running tests for Clostridium botulinum bacteria."

"And did you find any?" asked Keya eagerly.

Sujin shook his head. "The only source I've been able to discover is the hot sauce. The inspector and Inspector Sue were leaving to break the news to Doreen as I left to visit you."

"Poor woman," Keya sympathised. Then she asked more brightly, "Are you hungry? One of the nurses was telling me about a sweet French bistro with vegetarian options not far from here, in the Montpellier area of Cheltenham.

"Are you allowed out?" asked Sujin.

"Not on my own," Keya giggled. "But with a responsible adult."

Sujin found Keya's overnight bag and, one-handed, she searched through it for something more appropriate to wear for a night out than a pair of tracksuit bottoms.

She found a dress she'd forgotten all about. It was a green soft cotton shift dress with a V-neck and embroidered flowers down the side and around the bottom.

Sujin pulled the blue curtain around the bed and asked, "Shall I call a nurse?"

"No, I'm sure I can manage. I need to get used to coping one-handed for a while." Keya smiled resolutely at Sujin, who pulled the curtain around her bed and stood sentry on the other side.

Keya pulled her trousers down and stepped out of them. She tugged up her T-shirt and wriggled. She tugged a bit more and, "Oops. Sujin, I'm stuck. Can you help me?"

She felt a firm tug and the T-shirt rose above her head.

"Thank you," she said, grinning sheepishly. "Perhaps I'm not as able as I'd hoped. Can you help me with my dress?"

It was only then that Keya realised Sujin was standing awkwardly and trying but failing to avert his gaze from her … and she was standing in front of him, wearing only her bra and knickers.

She had the urge to laugh.

"Quickly, I'll get cold," although in truth the ward's large glass window had needed to have the blinds half-closed in the afternoon to prevent the sun shining through and heating the ward up too much.

"Um."

"Surely you've seen a half-naked woman before," Keya teased. Rather than embarrassed, she felt free and confident standing before Sujin, even with only one arm working.

"Not you," he muttered as he grabbed her dress from the bed.

"You'll need to roll it up from the bottom and then place it over my right arm and my head. I'm afraid you'll have to manoeuvre my left arm into the sleeve."

Sujin coloured as he robotically followed her instructions. The loose-fitting dress draped over her and Sujin stood back.

"Just the arm," Keya reminded him.

Sujin reluctantly stepped forward and lifted her arm. As he wrestled it into the dress's short sleeve, his body touched Keya's and he jumped. But then he leaned into her and she into him as her left arm finally obeyed and Sujin slipped it into the dress's sleeve.

Breathlessly, Sujin stepped back and looked at her. There was a different look in his eye now. One she hadn't seen for a long time from anyone looking at her and she felt a stirring within her, and her body was flushed with warmth.

Fanning her face with her hand and, for the first time, feeling self-conscious, she suggested, "Let's go. It's hot in here."

Neither she nor Sujin spoke until they stepped outside the hospital into the warm evening air.

"We need to turn right and follow the main road across the

junction. The restaurant is down one of the side streets," Keya remembered. She smiled invitingly at Sujin, and he smiled shyly back.

They started walking. As they approached the traffic lights, Sujin reached out and tentatively took her right hand. She slipped her hand into his and gave it a quick squeeze of consent.

Despite the events of the past few days, she felt a lightness as they walked, hand in hand, in the warm summer evening with white-painted two-storey classical buildings on either side.

"I think this is it," she said as they passed an upmarket hairdressing salon and stopped in front of a green shopfront with an array of plants in the window screening the customers inside from passers-by.

"Bistro Evelyn," said Sujin, looking up and reading the writing across the top of the shop front.

Inside, they were shown to a table for two in the corner, beside the leafy plants. It felt both exotic and private.

Keya chose a twice-baked cheese and spinach soufflé with a house salad.

"Do you mind if I have a steak?" Sujin asked.

"Of course not. I'm vegetarian, as it's how I was brought up, but I don't begrudge other people eating meat, and I do like fish. In fact, I might change my mind and have the salmon in a herby sauce with French beans," she said, considering the menu again. "It will be better for me than cheese."

"The omega-3 fatty acids will help your recovery, and so will the protein," Sujin agreed.

"You see, I knew there was a reason I invited you along," Keya teased.

Sujin looked down at the table. His embarrassment was palpable.

"You know earlier …"

"When I had no clothes on," Keya prompted.

A waiter cleared his throat. "Madam. Monsieur. Are you ready to order?"

Keya looked down at her menu and giggled.

"The steak, please, medium rare, with French fries, and Béarnaise sauce, but can I have it in a jug on the side?" Sujin asked, his face flushed.

"Certainly," the waiter replied in an approving tone.

"And the salmon for me please," Keya said, having composed herself.

"And to drink?"

"Do you have any of the French Bloom zero alcohol sparking rosé?"

"Of course, Monsieur."

Keya looked at the price of the bottle and gasped. It may not have alcohol in it, but it was still expensive. She looked up at Sujin, who was smiling tenderly at her.

"I think we have something to celebrate, don't we?" he asked.

"Our first date," Keya said.

"Yes, if we consider our evening at The Swan Hotel as a trial."

The waiter reappeared, popped open the bottle of pink fizz and poured two glasses.

Sujin raised his glass, and Keya lifted hers to it.

As they sat, leaning forward with their glasses touching, Sujin toasted, "To a bright future together."

"A bright future. Together," Keya repeated, smiling.

Sujin looked into her eyes and said, "When I saw you standing in the hospital earlier, I didn't know what to do. I was paralysed. You are so beautiful."

Keya's smile broadened. Although she was the one who was paralysed, nobody had called her beautiful for a long time.

CHAPTER THIRTY-EIGHT

Keya was still smiling to herself when she woke on Tuesday morning. The smell of disinfectant, partly masked by the aroma of Sujin's vase of summer flowers, and the efficient activity in the ward only made her evening out with Sujin feel all the more surreal.

They'd had a fabulous meal, washed down with the wonderfully expensive pink fizz, which they'd finished off with the theatrical performance of flaming Crepe Suzette.

And they'd talked over tea and coffee until they were the last ones in the restaurant.

Keya leaned back on her pillows and regarded the stained off-white ceiling.

They'd agreed to take things steady for the moment, as Keya needed to recover and she would still have the demands of both her police work and the cafe. But Sujin had urged her to accept Dotty's offer to accompany her on a trip to the Lake District.

"Are you ready for breakfast?" asked an orderly. "And you might want to ask a nurse to help you dress. Monday mornings are always busy in here as new patients come onto the ward from operations."

Dressed in her tracksuit bottoms and a fresh T-shirt, Keya sat up in bed eating a peach yoghurt - no strawberry this morning - as she watched the comings and goings on the ward. One of the elderly patients had been moved the previous evening and there was a gap where his bed had been.

"I hope you're thinking about our case," Inspector Evans remarked as he strode up to her bed.

"Inspector. This is a surprise."

"Yes, well, I've come with my cap in my hand, so to speak. I know you need your rest and recovery time, but we're almost done with Daisy Bentham's case."

"You think it was accidental, don't you?"

"That's the way the evidence is pointing. That Doreen Skinner got the recipe wrong and made a deadly batch of her hot sauce and both you and Daisy ate it, with tragic consequences."

Keya remembered being inside the standing stones and the voice that had been so insistent inside her head. "I still think there's more to this, sir."

"I thought you might, which is why I need your help. Do you feel up to returning to the station with me this morning?"

"If you'll provide lunch. The stuff they serve in here is dreadful. And some decent tea."

"Done. I've spoken to the ward sister, and they'll be busy all morning. You're due for physio this afternoon, but not with Laura. Sister said if you can remember to do your exercises you can skip that, but hopefully we won't need you for too long, and I can bring you back to rest this afternoon."

On the drive from Cheltenham to Cirencester, Keya asked Inspector Evans, "How was your interview with Doreen Skinner yesterday evening? I thought you were sending Warren with Inspector Sue."

"I was going to," agreed the inspector, "but since Doreen's sauce caused Daisy's death, as well as your illness, I wanted to look her in the eye."

"And do you think she's innocent?"

"I'm not sure. Probably. But she was too upset for me to read her. Distraught is actually the term I'd use. But then we had just told her she'd effectively killed her daughter."

Back at the station, Inspector Evans had to chaperone Keya to the team room after she'd been enthusiastically welcomed back by the duty sergeant, who'd then spent several minutes questioning her about her ordeal.

Word must have spread as other officers appeared until the inspector took charge and escorted her through the entrance and along the corridor to their team room.

Applause erupted as they walked in and beside her desk there were three balloons bobbing about, attached to ribbons which rose from a stand on the floor. A silver one had 'Welcome Back' printed on it.

She smiled gratefully, but thought the sentiment was premature. It was only as she'd entered the station that she realised it might be some time before she was officially passed fit enough to return to her police work.

As she approached her desk, she stopped and laughed. Sitting on her chair was a furry brown teddy bear wearing a black and white apron and a replica police hat.

"He's great, isn't he?" Ryan said. "Sujin brought him in this morning and asked Sue and me if we thought you'd like him. And when he heard you were coming into the station, he left him to welcome your return."

"And it is a relief to see you," Sue said, sitting behind her old desk.

Warren was seated at the other unallocated desk, and Stan was standing beside Ryan.

"The Chief Inspector wanted to greet you personally," Stan said, "but he's been called to a budget meeting."

Keya picked the teddy bear up with her right hand and placed him on her desk next to a pile of coloured envelopes. Looking down, she realised she'd struggle to open them. Even the simplest of tasks were going to prove difficult without the use of both arms.

But she mustn't think about that now. She was here to do a job.

"Sorry I'm late," Sujin said breathlessly as he entered the room. "I was just double checking all the data before we go through the case."

"I'll make the drinks while you settle Keya in," Stan said.

"Constable," said the inspector, addressing Warren. "Wheel out the spare chair from my office and give Sujin his old desk back. And then wheel out the whiteboard. It might be helpful to write some notes as we review the case."

CHAPTER THIRTY-NINE

"Is everyone ready?" asked Inspector Evans.

There was a murmur of consent.

Keya was sitting in her office chair with a cup of tea on her desk and one of Stan's missus' cheese scones, cut in half and buttered.

"We now know that Daisy Bentham died of botulinum poisoning after consuming hot sauce at lunchtime on the Sunday preceding her death."

Keya raised her right hand.

"Yes, Sergeant?"

"Has it been established that Daisy ate the hot sauce? She didn't usually."

"Yes," Inspector Evans confirmed. "Both Theo Watson and Zoe Bentham agreed she did. Apparently, they were joking that she couldn't handle spicy food, which is why she ate the sauce. And before you ask, she was the only one. Theo admitted he usually did, but he'd had spicy curry the night before and only added sour cream to his nachos and fajitas."

Inspector Evans stepped towards the white board which Warren had positioned in front of the wall, near the door. He wrote Daisy's name, the date of her death, and to one side hot sauce, which he linked by an arrow to Daisy's details.

Above the hot sauce he wrote Doreen Skinner and, below it, 'made the sauce'.

"Inspector Sue and I interviewed Doreen last night, and she was beside herself with grief. We didn't get anything useful out of her except that she admitted to making the hot sauce. So that's the only link we have. Doreen made the sauce which Daisy ate."

"Did she say she actually handed the bottle to Daisy or Theo?" Keya asked.

"Why is that important?" the inspector asked in an interested tone.

"Because I now remember that when I visited the bakery with Daisy, Ashley Ricketts came in and gave Daisy a bottle of the sauce. He said it was from Daisy's mum, but we only have his word for it."

"But according to your notes," Inspector Sue chimed in, "Ash was in love with Daisy, so why would he want to hurt her?"

"I think we're missing the point. Daisy didn't usually eat the sauce. Theo did. Surely, he was the intended victim?" reasoned Keya.

The room fell silent.

Eventually Inspector Evans said, "Point taken," as he wrote Theo Watson's name under Daisy's and added 'intended victim?'. Then he drew an arrow from the hot sauce to Theo's name.

"Why would Daisy's mum want to harm Theo?" Ryan asked.

"Because she was jealous. Daisy was happy in her relationship with a man who respected her and encouraged her in a new business venture. A very different experience from the one Doreen had experienced in her abusive marriages."

"But surely she'd be happy for Daisy?" Ryan pressed.

"You'd think so. But remember, Warren," Keya turned to look at the young constable, "how Doreen complained about her pokey cottage, while Daisy was living up at Mill House. She was definitely jealous of Daisy's garden."

"Unfortunately," Inspector Sue said ruefully, "people hurt those they are closest to. It's not unheard of for a parent to wound or injure a child, even a grown one. In fact, they're probably more likely to strike out at a grown child who is beyond their influence."

"Warren," Keya said again, "do you remember when I asked Doreen about her relationship with Daisy?"

"Yes, she winced when you first asked her, and the next time, she was defensive. You asked if they'd had an argument, but instead of answering she wanted to know who'd told you about an argument, and said they were lying. As if she knew someone had, and they'd snitched on her."

"But they hadn't and, rather than press her in her grief, I moved the questioning on. I should have asked who she thought had told me."

"I doubt she would have said," reflected Inspector Sue. "Doreen doesn't give away more information than she has to."

"I would put my money on Theo being the one who either witnessed an altercation or consoled Daisy after one. When Doreen arrived up at the standing stones, she blamed Theo for Daisy's death," Keya recalled.

"Why would she do that?" Ryan asked. "If she'd given them the dodgy sauce."

"Because he was alive and Daisy wasn't, and Doreen suspected, or knew, that Theo hadn't touched the sauce but had goaded Daisy into doing so."

Inspector Evans coughed. "We're heading far into the realm of conjecture. Sujin, is there anything scientific that you can add to the discussion?"

"Only that of all the items I tested, only the hot sauce carried the Clostridium botulinum bacteria. But that's not to say there wasn't something else which carried it, and the culprit got rid of it."

Inspector Evans frowned.

Keya didn't think that was what he wanted to hear. It just added more uncertainty to their case.

Ryan said, "I couldn't find anything unusual in Daisy's bank records. She received a basic salary from Stone Circle Flour, and she gave away half of it, split between her sister and both her parents."

"So Doreen suffered financially from Daisy's death. Which strengthens my case that she was targeting Theo, not Daisy."

"But wouldn't she be affected by Theo's death as well and …" Ryan began.

"Let's not rush down another rabbit hole," interjected Inspector Evans. "What about the phone records?"

"I'd say her relationship with her mother was strained. And she'd recently told Ashley in no uncertain terms that she was not interested in a relationship with him and that her future was with Theo," Keya replied.

Inspector Evan's wrote Ashley Ricketts' name on the board and under it, 'hot sauce courier' and a dotted line to Theo's name with jealous written above it.

"Anything else?" enquired the inspector.

"What about Daisy's father or sister?" Warren suggested nervously.

"Too lazy," Ryan responded. "And since Daisy was giving him money, he probably thought it was only a matter of time until she came back. And I don't think the sister has the presence of mind to concoct such a plan."

"Conjecture," called out Inspector Evans.

"I agree with Ryan," Keya said.

"Evidence?" Inspector Evans retorted.

"We've hardly enough to prove who committed the crime, never mind who didn't."

Inspector Evans wrote on the board, 'Dennis Bentham, Zoe Bentham, Aurora, Viv, Dr Reid, Dora?'

"Really, sir?" Keya questioned.

"As you've said, Sergeant, we don't have sufficient evidence to rule them out."

"You have missed off one name," Inspector Sue observed. "That of Theo Watson."

"Do you think he did it?" countered the Inspector.

"No, but we can't rule him out. And he did avoid the hot sauce again when Keya cooked lunch. I admit, if he was guilty, you'd expect him to get rid of the evidence, unless he thought he was being clever hiding the bottle in plain sight."

"Conjecture again, but I take your point," Inspector Evans accepted.

He wrote 'Theo Watson' on the board. Then he asked, "Is that it?"

"Of those we know about. I don't suppose you want to add Sir Anthony to the list," Inspector Sue suggested.

"No. I don't. Not without concrete evidence that he was involved. But I can't see him having anything to do with a bottle of homemade hot sauce." Inspector Evans capped his black marker pen and announced, "There you have it. As clear as mud. Or hot sauce."

“So what now?” Keya asked, wondering if her temporary release from the hospital was over.

“There is only one resource we have left,” Inspector Evans declared.

They all turned to him.

Did he have a magic solution Keya hadn’t thought about?

“To get them all in a room and look them in the eye. For you to look them in the eye, Sergeant, since you are also a victim of this crime.”

CHAPTER FORTY

Inspector Sue volunteered to contact all the suspects and arrange a meeting for the afternoon. "I'll start with Dr Reid and ask him if there is somewhere we can hold it in Lower Rollright," she told Keya and Inspector Evans.

Ryan and Warren had left to buy the team an early lunch, much to Keya's relief and appreciation for the inspector keeping his word. Sujin had said he needed to check something in his workroom, and Stan was seeing if anyone had requested files while he'd been in the morning meeting, since organising them was his official job.

Chief Inspector Greg poked his bald head round the door and, seeing the white board, asked cheerfully, "Are you close to resolving the case?"

"If we're not, sir," replied Inspector Evans, "then I doubt we'll ever be. But we are speaking to all those who knew the deceased again this afternoon."

"Very good." The chief inspector nodded his head and left. Keya thought he looked like a man with more pressing issues on his mind.

Inspector Evans strode up and down the room a couple of times and then stopped beside Keya's desk. "You should practise your physio exercises, or I'll be in trouble."

"I'll start by trying to open these envelopes," Keya replied.

"Do you have a paper knife?"

"No."

"Then let me fetch mine."

The inspector returned from his office with what looked like an old, possibly antique, silver paper knife with initials engraved on the handle.

"It was my mother's," he said. "Originally given to her by her mother. I keep it in the office to remember her by."

"Does the pain of losing someone become any less, sir?"

The inspector drew his lips together and shook his head. "No, and I don't think it ever will. I'll probably always carry a dull ache around with me. I know she was my mother and not my wife, but we lived together for so long. She was my soulmate. And that's why I feel a piece of me is missing."

Keya glanced at the names on the board and wondered which of them felt they'd lost part of their soul when Daisy died.

Keya realised again that even simple tasks were going to be challenging with only one arm working correctly. But finally she worked out a system whereby she used her right arm to place her left hand on an envelope, which provided enough pressure to allow her to slit the envelope open.

The first card she slipped out of its envelope had a giant colourful cake on the front and inside Happy Birthday had been crossed out and her employees at the cafe had each written encouraging notes. She even recognised the names of several regular customers who'd added their get well wishes.

The Wimsey family, Dotty, and Aunt Beanie, with Norman and Uncle Cliff's names inside, had also sent her upbeat cards with encouraging messages. She arranged them on her desk.

The rest of the team ate sandwiches for lunch while Keya and Inspector Sue shared a portion of asparagus and pea risotto served with a side salad.

"That do you?" asked Inspector Evans as Keya pierced the last pea in her brown cardboard takeaway container.

"Yes, sir. Delicious, and a welcome alternative to hospital food. But now I guess I'd better earn it."

"Solve this case and I'll buy everyone afternoon tea at your cafe."

Ryan and Warren looked delighted by the prospect, but Sujin warned, "But don't feel under pressure, Keya. You can't force the truth, and none of us wants you to have a relapse."

"Well said, Sujin," agreed the inspector, "but …"

"Dai," Inspector Sue warned, using Inspector Evans' Christian name. She gave him a look which clearly meant 'drop it'.

The whole team drove to Lower Rollright.

Sujin took Ryan and Keya, and although Ryan had offered Keya the front seat in Sujin's Skoda Yeti, she declined and climbed into the back. She squeezed in next to Sujin's bags of crime scene investigation kit, regarding the large fishing net and hockey stick lying on the floor.

"What's that metal rod?" asked Keya, as she carefully rested her feet on it, and noticed the metal cup on the other end.

"It's for retrieving golf balls or, in my case, hard to reach pieces of evidence."

They followed Inspector Evans, who had Inspector Sue sitting in the front seat of his car.

"Poor Warren. He looked petrified climbing into the back of the car with the two inspectors," commented Ryan.

"At least he's able to come. Poor Stan looked so disappointed at having to stay behind," Keya replied. "Although I'm not confident this will resolve the case."

As they drove past a pretty thatched cottage with a row of colourful flowers growing in front of a neatly trimmed hedge, Sujin said, "The final throw of the dice."

CHAPTER FORTY-ONE

Dr Reid was waiting for them outside Lower Rollrights's church hall. The hall and the church were located at the end of the lane which was also home to the Malt Shovel pub, Aurora's shop and Daisy's bakery.

"I've done as you requested. Dora's inside setting up and Theo should be arriving soon with Doreen and Ashley. I also thought I should inform Sir Anthony, although I doubt he'll come, and Dennis and Zoe, as they are Daisy's family."

Inspector Evans flattened his lips together in irritation.

"Cooee," came a voice from behind them, and Keya turned to see Aurora advancing up the lane, followed by black-haired Viv. As Aurora reached them, she panted, "I saw the police cars. Is this about Daisy?"

"It is Mrs …"

"Call me Aurora, and this is Viv. I'm dying to know what happened," and before anyone could stop them, the two women entered the single-storey stone church hall.

"My wife sends her apologies," said Dr Reid, "but someone has to manage the shop."

Dr Reid led the two inspectors inside the church hall and Keya was about to follow when she saw a cream van approaching. It parked beside the curb and Ashley Ricketts climbed out of the driver's side, and Doreen out of the passenger side.

As Ashley approached Keya, she asked, "Is Theo not with you?"

"He'll be here in a few minutes," Ashley replied.

"He wanted to walk and clear his head," Doreen added.

They all entered the hall, which had a raised stage at the far end. A circle of black metal chairs had been arranged on the varnished wooden floor.

Keya had the fleeting thought that they were all attending a seance, and that Daisy would speak to them through one of the attendees and identify her killer.

"Hi, Keya. How are you feeling?" Theo asked as he entered the hall and walked towards her. Although his face was flushed from his walk, he wasn't sweating or out of breath.

"Better than Friday," Keya admitted. "But I've only been allowed out of the hospital for the day. They say they want to keep an eye on me and make sure there are no complications."

"So you're better. No lingering side effects," Theo said, sounding relieved.

"I wouldn't say no side effects, but nothing permanent. I hope."

Inspector Evans cleared his throat. "Can everyone sit down, please?" Taking the lead, he sat on a chair with his back to the stage, facing the door, with Inspector Sue seated next to him. He'd instructed Ryan to sit near the entrance door and Warren to remain beside the door which led through to the kitchen and the hall's side door.

Keya and Sujin sat together, part way round the circle. Dr Reid, with Dora beside him, sat next to Inspector Evans, and Doreen placed herself next to Inspector Sue.

"Can we sit here?" Aurora asked, eyeing the empty seat beside Keya.

"Of course." Keya smiled back at her.

Ashley sat on his own, opposite the Inspector, and Keya understood why the inspector had wanted the two constables guarding the doors. Ashley looked ready to spring up and make his escape.

Theo sat on his own, opposite Keya and Sujin.

"I think that's everyone. Thank you for coming. I'm Inspector

Evans from Cirencester Police Station. Most of you have met my colleague, Inspector Sue."

"Hello," Inspector Sue said.

"And Sergeant Varma, who you may not realise, is also a victim of this crime."

Keya smiled ruefully and felt her cheeks burn.

"What happened to you?" Aurora whispered.

"I'm sure the inspector will elaborate soon," replied Keya in a low voice.

The entrance door opened, and an unshaven Dennis Bentham entered, followed by Zoe, who was hiding behind him.

"Zoe, come and sit with us," Aurora invited. She whispered something to Viv, who shuffled across to sit beside Ashley, leaving a free seat which Zoe hurriedly took.

Dennis slumped in a chair on the other side of Ashley, stretched out his legs, and folded his arms.

"As I was saying, thank you for coming," repeated Inspector Evans. "We believe we now know how Daisy died."

"I didn't mean to kill her!" Doreen cried in a shrill voice.

The inhabitants of Lower Rollright all stared at her.

Inspector Sue whispered something in the inspector's ear.

"Mrs Skinner, if you'll just be patient, we'll find out exactly what happened to Daisy. Let me introduce the other member of our team, Sujin Kerr, who is our crime scene and forensic expert."

Sujin raised his hand in acknowledgement.

"Sujin has discovered that Daisy, and Sergeant Varma, both suffered from botulinum poisoning after eating some of Mrs Skinner's hot sauce."

Beside Keya, Aurora gasped.

"Aah" cried Doreen, sounding like a wounded animal.

The inspector pressed on. "After Sergeant Varma was admitted to hospital and her illness was diagnosed, Sujin tested everything she'd eaten, including the hot sauce in the fridge at Mill House. It tested positive for the Clostridium botulinum bacteria, which produces the poisonous toxin."

"What were you doing at Mill House?" Aurora whispered.

"My job," Keya murmured, noting that Aurora hadn't asked about her stint in hospital.

"But Daisy doesn't eat hot sauce," Ashley protested.

"What?" cried Doreen. "Then who does?"

"Me," Theo answered quietly. Everyone sat still as they listened to him. "I'm the one who likes the sauce, and Zoe sometimes when she's eating with us. But last Sunday I didn't have any, because of the curry I'd eaten the night before, but Zoe and I dared Daisy to try it. And she did." Theo gulped and blinked his eyes.

"Exactly," Inspector Evans continued. "And I'm afraid that proved fatal."

"But Daisy died on the summer solstice," Dora piped up in a thin voice. "I saw her dancing round the fire the evening before and thought how carefree and happy she looked." Dora sounded both wistful and jealous.

Sujin coughed. "If I may, Inspector?"

"Go ahead, Sujin."

"Botulism, or botulinum poisoning, happens sometime after ingesting the toxins. On average, twenty-four to thirty-six hours after, but it can be four hours, or eight days. Indeed, there are recorded cases where the source of the poisoning can be traced back to thirty days before the symptoms became apparent."

"Which means it is logical for Daisy to have eaten something containing the toxins on Sunday lunchtime, and to have died on Tuesday night," considered Dr Reid.

"That's correct," Sujin agreed.

Next to Keya, Aurora was fidgeting. Then she blurted, "But why did you give Daisy and Theo a bottle of contaminated sauce, Doreen? And what about the others on sale at the Rollright Stores? Are they also deadly?"

Several people, including Doreen and Dora, winced.

"I did not give my own daughter a bottle of contaminated sauce. And there is nothing wrong with the ones I sell through Mrs Reid's store. Don't go spreading rumours that there is, Aurora. Or that I deliberately poisoned my daughter. He must have put something in the bottle. That's why he didn't have any," Doreen sobbed, as she pointed a finger at Theo.

"Why do you think Theo harmed Daisy?" asked Keya in a quiet voice.

Doreen gulped back sobs. "Who else would have wanted to? He took her away from her family."

"But that's not true, is it, Dennis?" Keya stared at Daisy's unkempt father. "You threw her out. Theo was the one who provided her with a place to live. Who supported her. From all that I've seen and heard, Theo and Daisy were about to start on a bright future together. And start a family."

Doreen sobbed louder and Zoe cried out before curling up in a ball on her chair.

Viv placed a comforting arm around her.

Beside Keya, Aurora made a harrumphing sound before she declared, "I don't understand about the sauce. Doreen says there was nothing wrong with it when there clearly was. I don't suppose you can inject the poison into a bottle?"

Sujin considered the remark before replying, "I suppose you could, but not this bottle. The toxins were part of the mixture and had clearly originated with the production process."

Aurora turned to Doreen and said, "So you did give Daisy a bottle of poisoned sauce."

"No, I didn't," Doreen protested vehemently. "I'm well aware that botulism can come from improperly prepared vegetables. That's why I threw away one mixture this year. I was bottling it and realised it was all gassy. That's a sign something is wrong."

Doreen turned to Dora and said, "You were with me when it happened. Don't you remember? I was furious that I'd wasted an entire batch and I'd have to start again."

"I'm not sure," Dora replied, blushing and fidgeting with her hands.

"What did you do with the wasted batch?" Keya asked Doreen.

Doreen sighed. "I had to throw it all away, and empty the bottles I'd already filled …" Her voice trailed off and she screwed her face up in concentration.

"What is it?" Keya probed gently.

"I thought at the time that I was a bottle short. That I'd filled two and whilst pouring the mixture into the third, I realised it wasn't right. But I only emptied and sterilised two bottles."

"So what happened to the third?" Inspector Evans demanded as Keya's attention was drawn back to Dora.

The thin, grey-haired woman, who Keya knew had a defiant, jealous side to her, had pinned her arms across her stomach. She was still flushed and looked exceedingly uncomfortable. And of course, she was there when Doreen was bottling the mixture.

"Dora," Keya said in a clear, no-nonsense tone. "Did you take a bottle of the spoiled hot sauce?"

"Yes," squealed Dora. "But I didn't give it to Daisy." Her face and her voice hardened as she admitted, "I wanted to. I thought about it. With her and Theo out of the way, I could move back to Mill House. To my beloved garden."

"Dora!" Aurora admonished.

Dora's voice became high pitched again as she protested, "But I didn't. I knew it was wrong. Not Christian-like behaviour." She used her arms to hug herself.

"But you did take a bottle?" Keya confirmed.

Dora nodded.

"So, where is it now?"

"On a shelf in the storeroom at the shop."

Dr Reid gasped.

"I meant to throw it away," Dora wailed. "But I didn't get round to it. I'll do it as soon as this meeting is over."

Beside Inspector Evans, Dr Reid had an ashen pallor.

"What's wrong, Dr Reid?" Keya asked.

"I picked a bottle off the storeroom shelf and gave it to Ashley after he dropped a bottle in the shop. It made a dreadful mess. Stained the floor, didn't it Dora? I know you've tried several times to scrub it clean."

Ashley's face became as red as a bottle of the infamous hot sauce. "I did drop a bottle. But it wasn't from the shelf. It was the one Doreen gave me to give to Daisy."

"Oh." Dr Reid sounded uncertain.

"The bottle you gave Ashley, Dr Reid. Do you think it was the contaminated one Dora left?" Keya asked.

"I don't know," Dr Reid admitted.

"Then we need to find out," Inspector Evans declared. "Constable Ryan."

"Yes, sir," answered Ryan, who'd left his seat beside the entrance door and moved closer to the circle of chairs as the discussion had developed.

"Please escort Miss Potts to the village store to locate the missing bottle of contaminated hot sauce."

"Yes, sir."

CHAPTER FORTY-TWO

Ryan left with Dora, who scuttled out of the church hall.

Beside Keya, Aurora and Viv consoled Zoe.

Keya had been alert during the discussion, but now she felt a heaviness starting to creep through her. A tiredness from the exertion, and also a dull feeling that Daisy's death was pointless.

She looked up as Theo approached her.

"I'm so sorry that you've been caught up in our village issues, and that you were poisoned at my house. I feel dreadful. You were only trying to help me."

"I'll be fine," Keya reassured him. She refrained from adding that at least she was still alive.

Inspector Sue was leaning over and consoling a sobbing Doreen, while Inspector Evans stood facing Dr Reid as they both discussed Sir Anthony in loud voices.

Dennis Bentham sat on his own, seemingly oblivious to all that was happening around him.

"Do I still need to stand by the kitchen door?" asked Warren as he joined Theo and Keya.

"Can you keep an eye on Ashley Ricketts? He looks ready to do a runner," Keya said.

They all stared at Ashley, whose gaze darted around the room.

Then his phone pinged, and he looked down at it and started tapping it with his thumbs.

It was another ten minutes before a tear-stained Dora and a glum-looking Ryan returned, accompanied by a concerned-looking Mrs Reid.

"I've shut the shop," Mrs Reid told her husband, "while we get to the bottom of this business. Is it true that we sold the bottle of hot sauce which poisoned Daisy Bentham?"

All the police officers looked towards Ryan.

"Constable?" Inspector Evans questioned.

"The bottle wasn't there," Ryan replied.

"Dora put it on the top shelf, Silas. Next to the packs of postcards."

Dr Reid swallowed before replying. "That's right. I took that bottle and also a pack of postcards to replenish the stock in the back room after a busy few days of visiting tourists."

Inspector Evans cleared his throat. "Please, can you all take your seats again?"

A hush fell, as everyone did as instructed. Mrs Reid sat down next to her husband and looked round the group with a distressed expression on her face.

"Ashley, what did you do with the bottle of hot sauce that Dr Reid sold you?" Inspector Evans asked.

"I left it with Daisy at the bakery. The morning when you were visiting." Ashley looked at Keya.

"I do remember you coming into the shop as Daisy was making my sandwich," Keya confirmed.

"So that's how a bottle of contaminated but inconspicuous hot sauce made its way from Mrs Skinner's kitchen to the dining table at Mill House, and poisoned two people. One of them fatally," Inspector Evans concluded.

Keya heard gasps, gulps, and a collective intake of breath.

Dennis Bentham looked up and asked slowly, "So who's responsible for my daughter's death?"

"While I feel like charging you all with gross negligence

manslaughter for causing the death of a beautiful young woman," growled Inspector Evans, "I expect the coroner will return a verdict of accidental death."

Again, Keya was aware of an intake of breath, and a collective sigh.

Inspector Evans fixed his gaze on Doreen Skinner as he said, "I recommend you think seriously about continuing to make your hot sauce in a domestic environment, especially when other people are around."

His attention turned to Dora, who glanced up at him with a stricken expression.

"It was your malicious thoughts of harming Daisy, and your action in stealing the spoilt bottle of hot sauce, which were the catalyst for this tragedy."

"But ..." squeaked Dora.

"I'm not interested in excuses. You need to think how you can best atone for what you did," said the inspector gravely.

Dora bowed her head.

"And Ashley." The inspector spoke to the young man. "You need to be truthful in the future, however hard it is, otherwise the consequences may be far more serious than you can imagine."

He turned to the group as a whole and said, "And you should all apologise for the pain and suffering you've caused Sergeant Varma. She may pretend everything is all right, but if her left arm remains paralysed, she may lose her job and her business."

Keya felt all eyes turn to her as the impact of the inspector's words hit home.

He was right. She could lose everything.

Beside her, Sujin placed his arm around her protectively.

Despite it all, she smiled. Not everything.

CHAPTER FORTY-THREE

"The doctor shouldn't have allowed you to go out today. You're exhausted," a nurse scolded as she helped Keya into her pyjamas on Tuesday evening.

Keya certainly felt wiped out, but she wouldn't have missed the afternoon's meeting. It gave her closure about Daisy's death and her poisoning, however unsatisfactory that was.

Aurora and Viv had promised to keep an eye on Theo, and Viv had even said she might ask about taking over the bakery. She enjoyed helping Aurora, but the shop was barely profitable enough to support them both.

Keya had told her to be in touch if she did, as the Waterwheel Cafe and Deli would certainly be interested in stocking and using the bakery's products.

"Here's your tea," said the nurse as she pulled back the blue curtain.

Keya tried to look enthusiastic as a grey plastic plate of limp egg sandwiches was placed on her portable table. But when the orderly left, she reached under her pillow and removed a plastic container of couscous salad, which Sujin had bought for her before she'd returned to the hospital.

Beside her, a lady with neat, bobbed, white hair laughed. "I don't blame you, dear. I'm here because of an issue with my digestion, and the food they serve is hardly going to help. Now I noticed that young police officer who escorted you here. Have you done something naughty?"

Keya smiled. Her stay in the hospital was going to be far more fun with her new neighbour.

Ryan came with Zivah to visit on Wednesday morning.

"Ryan gave me a lift," Zivah said, "and smuggled me in. Otherwise I wouldn't be able to visit as I'm at the cafe this afternoon and then picking Kaami up from Mum's when I've finished. Feeding, bathing, and putting him to bed takes hours, so I'd also miss this evening's visiting hours. But how long are you going to be in here?"

"A few more days, I think. They're concerned that I exhausted myself yesterday, but I needed to find out what happened to Daisy."

"Ryan told me all about it." Zivah glanced at Ryan.

"It's terrible," she continued. "And in a small community like that. They must all be devastated. But then people aren't as kind, considerate, and tolerant as they should be. Look at old Mr Shipton, who lives next to the Clutterbucks' farm where Ryan lives. The residents in the houses opposite treat him dreadfully, even though they've only just moved in, and he's lived in his bungalow for years."

Keya looked at Ryan and asked, "Is it something you need to get involved in?"

"I have tried to mediate, in an unofficial capacity. I can see the new residents' point of view. But they knew Mr Shipton's place was a mess before they bought their executive homes."

"I suspect the development company told them they were in the process of buying the property to build more houses, as I know they've tried to do, but Mr Shipton has no intention of leaving," Zivah explained.

Keya enjoyed the discussion about the residents on Zivah's street and she was pleased Ryan was close by to keep an eye on her sister.

"How was your weekend trip along the Cotswold Way?" Keya asked.

"Good. It wasn't too hot on Sunday, so we ran the route in a reasonable time. And we'll complete the final leg this Sunday, as long as Millie can organise someone to cover for her at the cafe."

Zivah must have seen the concern on Keya's face as she said, "But don't worry. We'll sort something out."

There it was again. She should be organising and arranging shifts in her cafe. Not relying on others to do it for her.

Ryan cleared his throat and said, "And I came this morning to discuss your rural engagement commitments, which I'm taking over this week. There's the school prize-giving, and what are your thoughts on security and our involvement at The Big Feastival?"

On Wednesday evening, Ryan and Warren accompanied Sujin to Cheltenham Hospital. Sujin collected Keya from the ward, and they sat at a table downstairs in the cafe and ordered a light supper.

"You're still with the team?" Keya said to Warren.

"At least until you return to work. And we've solved a major case, haven't we, Ryan?"

Sujin sat back, smiling.

"Daisy's?" Keya asked in confusion.

"No. We caught the crop circle creators." Warren proudly thrust his chest out.

"How?" Keya demanded, intrigued.

"It was Ashley Ricketts," Ryan explained. "Some of his drinking mates were boasting about it in the pub. Ash admitted he normally eggs them on, but after what happened to Daisy, he thought he better report it in case someone else was injured."

"So we were waiting for them at a field near Upper Oddington, and we caught them in the act!" Warren beamed.

"When?" Keya asked.

"Half past four this morning!" Warren admitted.

"You must be exhausted."

"They're young," Sujin reasoned, as Warren yawned.

"We have tomorrow off, don't we, Ryan?" Warren said.

"Why didn't you tell me about this when you visited earlier, Ryan?" Keya asked.

Looking sheepish, he replied, "I knew Warren wanted to tell you and he was processing the suspects when Zivah and I visited. And I might have the morning off, but I'm handing out prizes at the school sports day tomorrow afternoon. I think I'll go for a long bike ride in the morning. That'll energise me," Ryan said.

Warren gave him a sideways glance and muttered, "Not my idea of resting. But at least we have afternoon tea to look forward to at your cafe on Thursday, Keya. The inspector's treating us."

"I'm glad he kept his word, and I'm sorry I can't join you. What about you, Sujin?" Keya asked.

"I'm working with Inspector Sue on a missing person's case for head office in Gloucester. Inspector Unwin sends his regards, by the way."

"Say hi, if you see him again."

Sujin regarded her before asking, "He's a good-looking guy, were you and he ..."

"Oh, no! He did have his eye on Dotty for a while, but ... well, that's another story."

On Thursday, Dotty arrived as soon as afternoon visiting hours began.

The two of them chatted with Keya's entertaining neighbour until a nurse arrived and said respectfully to the elderly lady, "Dr Lewis, are you ready to go?"

"I'll miss her," Keya said as an orderly stripped the sheets on the now empty bed next to her. "None of the other patients say or do anything."

She looked at Dotty and asked, "How are things going with you? Did you visit the Lake District?"

"I did. It's a long drive, but beautiful once you get there. And the project is very exciting. I wasn't sure I'd be up to it but I think I can manage. I'm not in charge of all the furnishings, but I am sourcing quality items to create a luxury experience. And the owner wants different themes in different rooms. I'm putting together some thoughts at the moment, and then I'll need to visit galleries and auction houses in London. Hopefully, I can also source some pieces locally. You can help me when you've recovered."

"I've got enough to do. But I should have some time off from police work because of my condition. To tell you the truth, it's a relief. Sujin is right. I need to take a break and reassess my priorities. I want to be fully involved in the cafe and deli, rather than relying on everyone else's help. Things have run away with me lately."

"And your arm?" Dotty asked, directly.

"The feeling is back at the top and I can still wriggle my fingers so the doctors are confident both feeling and movement will return, but it is going to take time."

"And when will you be discharged?"

"I'm waiting to hear. Hopefully this evening or tomorrow morning. And then when I've sorted things out, I would like to visit the Lake District with you."

"That's fantastic. We'll have such fun. I've pencilled it in for the second week in July, before the schools break up, but with enough time before then for me to agree to the themes and source some items."

"Then I'll be able to help Gilly with the outdoor cinema night. And how are the plans for Gilly's party?"

"It's all slotting into place. Everyone's helping out, and I still don't think Gilly knows about it. But I'll be amazed if we keep it a secret until the night."

CHAPTER FORTY-FOUR

Keya was discharged from Cheltenham Hospital after lunch on Friday.

She'd had to wait around for the doctor's checks and the paperwork, and finally for Sujin to collect her.

"Sorry I'm late," Sujin said as he approached her space in the ward. She was sitting in a chair beside her stripped hospital bed, wearing a simple floral shift-style dress which was perfect for the sunny weather outside.

The sun's rays had begun heating up the ward, so the nurses had closed the blinds, but Keya longed to feel the sun on her face.

"Is that everything?" Sujin asked, eyeing her bags, which consisted of her overnight bag and several plastic carrier bags of additional clothes, Dotty's cookbook, and some of the magazines she'd been given.

"Yes, but is it too much?"

"Not if you help." Sujin lifted the strap of the overnight bag onto his shoulder and picked up two carrier bags.

Keya had already thanked the staff, but as she carried the third carrier bag out of the ward, she said a final goodbye to two of the nurses and followed Sujin along the hospital corridors.

As she climbed into Sujin's car, she asked, "Are you taking me to the station or home?"

"Neither. I have a surprise for you first."

Keya wasn't sure if she wanted a surprise, but then she wasn't certain what she wanted to do.

Home and her little cottage would be great for a while, but she needed to get stuck into something. Like taking back control of her cafe. She'd wanted to start cooking and baking again, but that wasn't possible at the moment with her paralysed left arm.

"You're very quiet. Is everything OK?" asked Sujin as he switched on the engine.

"I was thinking about what I should do now. What I actually can do. Because it's not working in the kitchen at the cafe with my arm as it is. But equally, I don't want to be stuck at home. And what am I going to do for transport?"

This was the first time Keya had considered the issue of driving. There was no way she could drive her Polo; it was a manual. She presumed if her arm didn't get better ... but she wasn't going to think about that.

"Dotty and I have discussed it. I hope you don't mind," Sujin added as they drove through Cheltenham.

"And while I'd love you to come and live with me, I think it's a bit forward and I don't want to rush you. But Dotty has a spare room, and so does Aunt Beanie in the main farmhouse, so you can stay with either of them."

So much for spending time in her cottage.

"But we also know you'll want to spend some time at home, even if it's only to recover from the last few weeks, so Ryan, Dotty and I are happy to provide a chauffeur service."

"That's really kind, thank you. But you and Ryan have work, and Dotty is still studying, and she's taken on a new project. Can I think about it?"

"Of course."

"And where are we going? This route looks familiar."

Sujin grinned. "Nearly there."

He parked in one of the new spaces at the side of the Waterwheel Cafe.

"Inspector Evan's afternoon tea," said Keya, realising why they were at her cafe.

"You didn't think we'd let you miss out, did you?" Sujin opened the door, and Keya climbed out.

As they approached the deli, Maitri ran out and gave Keya a huge hug. "I'm so happy to see you, and I thought, if you need a taxi service to the cafe, I can pick you up and drop you off on my way to and from work."

"That might work, thanks," Keya replied, starting to feel overwhelmed by the offers of help.

Several regular customers greeted her as she walked along the path to the old mill building.

A few ladies were out in the sun, but most customers were enjoying the warmth while remaining under the shade of the new wooden-framed structure and its extended awning.

As she stepped through the patio doors into the main cafe area, a ripple of applause started and increased in volume.

Feeling her cheeks burn, she walked towards a large table where Inspector Evans was sitting, wearing his brown suit and a satisfied expression on his face.

"We're all here. Excellent," said the Inspector as Sujin pulled out a chair for Keya, and she sat down between Ryan and the inspector. Sujin sat opposite her, next to Warren, and Stan looked delighted to be present, sitting at the end of the table.

"Inspector Sue?" Keya asked.

"She sends her apologies, but she's working on a missing person case for head office."

"Hi, Keya," Millie greeted her as she placed a tray on the table and started removing cups and saucers.

Keya had the urge to help, but she felt awkward not being fully mobile.

"And it's the afternoon tea for six, with a vegetarian selection," checked Millie.

"That's right," Inspector Evans replied.

The inspector politely asked Keya about her stay in hospital and how her arm was.

"You've been signed off on sick leave for the moment while you recover. We'll monitor the progress with your arm, but honestly, I think you need a break."

So everyone kept telling her, but she knew they were right. She would miss the camaraderie of the station and, in particular, her team room. "Who'll take over my rural engagement duties?" she asked.

"Constable Jenkins. He was a little awkward yesterday at the school prize-giving, but I understand The Big Feastival were very grateful for his input this morning. Warren can cover some of his other duties, and I also want Ryan to spend time in some of the other departments and revise for his sergeants' exams."

"Which I said I'd help him with. And let's hope it's not too busy over the summer."

"There are plenty of people who can assist Constable Ryan, and a peaceful summer is a nice thought, Sergeant. But there'll always be something." Inspector Evans looked up and, once again, smiled with satisfaction.

Millie and Alison were approaching their table, each carrying stacked cake stands filled with dainty sandwiches, pastries, and cakes.

The inspector leaned towards Keya and confided, "I do like your cafe."

CHAPTER FORTY-FIVE

Keya was delighted to feel useful the following Thursday as she helped Dotty and Aunt Beanie decorate and prepare the cafe for Gilly's birthday.

Despite her protests, Gilly had allowed Dr Peter to take her away for the afternoon so she couldn't wander into the cafe or hear whispers about the party from stallholders in the antique centre.

Aunt Beanie handed Keya a list. "These are the deliveries we're expecting today."

Keya looked down at it. There were balloons, a drinks delivery and, of course, the birthday cake.

Keya knew Monica had offered to provide the cake, but Aunt Beanie had told her she had enough to do with the cafe and food for the party, and had one ordered from elsewhere. Keya hoped Monica wasn't too put out.

Later, Keya helped Dotty hang bunting by either holding the step ladder with her right hand or passing up the end of a string of colourful pennants.

"It looks great, doesn't it?" Dotty enthused as Millie escorted the last of the cafe customers to the main door. "Now we need to rearrange the tables and chairs."

Sujin arrived as the reorganisation was taking place.

"Everything OK?" he asked Keya with a look of concern.

"Fine," she replied. And when he still looked at her with a worried expression, she reiterated. "I'm OK. Honestly. It's just frustrating at times not to be able to do everything I've previously taken for granted."

Sujin squeezed her hand. "I understand."

"Happy birthday, dear Gilly. Happy birthday to you," all the guests sang as Gilly stepped into the cafe accompanied by Dr Peter, Thomas, and Olivia. Gilly raised her hands to her mouth and when the singing stopped, she turned to Dr Peter and kissed him, before hugging both of her children.

Dotty and Keya watched as Millie handed Gilly and Dr Peter glasses of prosecco.

The other guests raised their glasses and chorused, "To Gilly."

Gilly was dressed in a green velvet dress with a pair of kitten heel shoes, and she looked very elegant. A far cry from the bare-footed woman having an existential crisis on the river bank a few weeks earlier.

As Gilly greeted her guests enthusiastically, Dotty, who was standing next to Keya, said, "It looks fabulous in here. Maybe you can add evening events and venue hire to the cafe's website."

"Not at the moment. We have enough to do." But Keya looked proudly around the cafe and at the food Monica, Mick, and Alison were placing on the buffet table. "But you're right, we should consider evening events, as it does look great. Can you take some photos in case we need some future marketing material?"

The future.

Who knew what it would bring?

Hot Chocolate and A Festive Fatality

Does being on sick leave give Keya more time for her cafe?

And what happens when Zivah's neighbours start quarrelling, and Cirencester Police Station comes under review?

Will Keya finally have to choose between her police work and the Waterwheel Cafe? And where does Sujin fit into her life?

Find out in Hot Chocolate and A Festive Fatality

Halloween Parade Peril

Keya and Sujin travel with the Celtic Twisters to Ireland. But when one of the band members dies at a Halloween Parade, they are drawn into the investigation with their friend and amateur sleuth, Dotty Sayers.

Find out how they work together to solve the case.

Hour is Come

Would you like to read Keya's first case with her friend Dotty? And discover how The Waterwheel Cafe and Dotty Sayers Antique Mystery series began?

Find out and download *Hour is Come,* which is yours to keep when you sign up to my newsletter for updates.

Claim your copy of Hour is Come

For more information visit VictoriaTait.com

UNTITLED

Manufactured by Amazon.ca
Acheson, AB

33714884R00114